FLIRTING WITH THE FORBIDDEN

SUBMITTING TO MY STEPBROTHER
BOOK FIVE

M. FRANCIS HASTINGS

To my very patient fans. I hope you enjoy reading it as much as I enjoyed writing it!

CONTENTS

1. Sophomore Problems	1
2. Thunderstruck	9
3. The Enemy of My Enemy	17
4. Bumper Cars	23
5. Another Farm	31
6. Jake's Friend	39
7. Texas Bound	47
8. Walkin' Around Money	55
9. Ibra-Whose-It	63
10. Anywhere But Here	69
11. Back with Hoot	77
12. Sublime	85
13. Big Boy	87
14. Sweet Pink Bottom	95
15. Up All Night	103
16. Restraint	111
17. Shut Up, Hank	119
18. A Special Kind of Prejudice	127
19. All In	135
20. A Space in My Heart	141
21. Shattered World	149
22. Care	157
23. Hell's Bells	165
24. Faking Sleep	171
25. Judgment	179
26. Bonus Chapter: Trouble	187
Also by M. Francis Hastings	195

1
SOPHOMORE PROBLEMS

McKenzie

I was just opening up my e-mail when my mother burst through the door. "Mom!" I cried. "Don't you kn—?" My complaint died on my lips when I saw how pale she was.

"McKenzie," she wheezed. Mom must have flown up the stairs. "You need to pack and go back to school."

"What?" I replied, closing the cover on my iPad. "Why? What's going on?"

"*Now!*" she all but screamed.

She was scared. Jocelyn Ann Kent, who I had never seen rattled in all my life, was absolutely terrified. "Mom?" I asked worriedly.

"No questions. Just pack. Take Billy's truck. He'll go pick it up later," she said, already rifling through my drawers and throwing things into my suitcase.

Most of the stuff she was choosing was stuff I'd been planning to leave behind, but she was so desperately afraid, I wasn't going to argue. I could always come back and get my stuff when... whatever this was... passed. "Okay," I responded slowly. "Okay. When's he going to come get it?"

"I don't know. A day? A week? It doesn't matter," my mother grunted, tossing in half my sock drawer.

"Even a day is going to cost a fortune in parking!" I protested. "I can't let Uncle Billy—"

"Don't argue with me," she snapped.

I closed my mouth. She'd never used that tone with me before.

She stopped packing, and her eyes welled up. "I love you, sweetie," she whispered, grabbing me suddenly in a strong hug. "I love you so much."

"Mom, please tell me what's going on," I begged, a sick feeling settling in my stomach.

"I can't. You need to leave. We'll contact you when we can," she said, handing my suitcase to me.

Pretty sure it was full of socks and zero underwear, I still took it and followed Mom out of my room and down the back stairs. I could still hear Dad talking to someone at the front door.

"Oh. I left the cereal…" I began.

"Forget the cereal. I'll take care of the cereal." My mother took a keychain down off the hook by the back door and pressed it into my hands. "Take Billy's truck. Go back to the U. Pretend like nothing's happened. Do you understand?"

I swallowed and nodded. "Okay." I opened the door and started outside, carrying my suitcase instead of rolling it so it didn't make noise. I dropped it in the back of the cab of Uncle Billy's truck then got behind the wheel.

There was an unfamiliar car in the wide dirt circle that served as parking between the house and the barn. Though 'car' was an understatement. It was a Lamborghini. I wondered who in their right mind would drive a car like that down a dirt road.

Whoever it was, it wasn't a salesperson or a political campaign canvasser. I knew that much. I quickly memorized the license plate—I had a photographic memory—and then fired up the truck and took off.

The dark-haired man in a nice suit who was standing at the door with my father turned his head, but I didn't see his face, and I didn't think he saw mine. I peeled out of the driveway, kicking rocks up to ping off his Lamborghini.

When I looked in the rearview mirror, I saw my mother coming around the side of the house with two duffel bags.

That was the last I saw of her.

* * *

CHEMISTRY WAS IMPOSSIBLE, BOTH INSIDE AND OUTSIDE OF CLASS. Somehow, I'd ended up in a wing of girls who were at the U to get their MRS degrees—or 'missus' for those who didn't get the joke. Basically a bunch of women who'd enrolled in college with the intention of marrying a doctor, lawyer, dentist, etc. with little to no intention of earning a degree themselves.

I couldn't believe, in my sophomore year, I was still being housed with them. I was even in a different dorm building! But since I was still in the quad, I supposed it was inevitable that transferring from Frontier to Centennial wasn't going to make a damn bit of difference.

Next year, I was staying in the Comstock building for sure.

"You know what?" My blonde, willowy roommate named Stacey sighed as I tried to do my chemistry homework. "I think I'd like to do laundry for the rest of my life."

I blinked at her. Just days ago, I'd been helping her with her remedial English paper. In return, she'd held a rager in our room over the weekend and allowed someone to spill beer all over my lofted bed. I didn't even want to know what else had happened on that bed, but there was a suspicious white stain on my blanket that hadn't come out in the wash.

"What?" she grumped, looking back at me. "I know Alex is just days away from asking me to marry him."

"Alex?" So it was Alex this week.

"Oh, you haven't met him. That's right. I had him over, over the weekend. He's staying tonight. He just had to pick up some more stuff," she said.

Here I was trying to pretend my parents hadn't disappeared and that I was just being studious while I was internally freaking out. And now she was going to move another man into our 10x10 dorm.

Usually, I'd have been quiet about it. Usually. But I was on the last fraying thread of my last nerve. "Were you going to ask me about that?"

"Huh?" Stacey asked, her blue eyes going wide with confusion.

"I don't want him here. In fact, you can cancel any other guys staying with us. If you want to go stay with him, that's fine, but I didn't sign up for two roommates in a 10x10 space," I said.

"Hey, you can't tell me what to do!" she huffed, glaring at me.

I glared right back. "No, I can't. But the RA can, and I've had it with you. This isn't a hostel. I get to feel comfortable in my own living space and not worry about your asshole boyfriends seeing me naked. I'm not going to put up with it anymore."

After a while, she couldn't meet my glare anymore. "Fine, whatever," she muttered at her laundry basket.

Knowing her, I was going to find something unpleasant in my bed later or have pop 'accidentally' spilled on my laptop. But for now, I felt pretty good. Aside from the fact my parents were missing and Uncle Billy, Uncle Jake, and Uncle Horace had all forbidden me from contacting them from anything other than a pay phone. I hadn't even known pay phones still existed!

I went back to chemistry, the numbers all swimming around my lab homework. A week ago, I could do this. A week ago, I'd have been all over this.

Now?

I could barely add two plus two.

Stacey sniffed and put her laundry away then stormed out of our dorm room, across the hall to Kelly, her best friend and minion, to complain about me. I couldn't muster the energy to care.

The door was open to the hallway, and I could see some more of the MRS Brigade, or as I liked to call them, TWITs (Trophy-Wives-In-Training) gathering in Kelly's dorm. I had a feeling this was going to lead to something bad.

"Fine, whatever," I muttered, echoing Stacey's earlier sentiment. I had bigger things to worry about than whether or not I found a used condom under my pillow tonight.

I glanced up several times as I worked on my chemistry lab write-up. The TWITs kept looking over at me and whispering. Finally, the entire posse of them started across the hall.

"Let me guess," I said before any of them could open their mouths. "Snitches get stitches and end up in ditches?"

The TWIT collective stared at me, not comprehending.

"We've decided Alex gets to stay," Stacey announced, finally just forging ahead.

"You did? That's nice. And again I say, 'no.' Unless he wants to stay with Kelly." I turned in my chair. "In fact, why don't you *both* stay there? She has a couch, and I'm *sure* she'd just *love* to hear the two of you going at it all night."

"You don't get to say, 'no.' We voted," she replied confidently.

I rose. "You can go ahead and tell that to the RA."

"Oh come *on*, McKenzie. Don't be a bitch," she griped. "It's just until he proposes."

I swallowed a retort about buying the cow when he's getting the milk for free. She was a vindictive idiot, but the idiot part wasn't her fault, and I wasn't going to be spiteful. That would be stooping to her level. "He's not staying here."

"Ugh!" She folded her arms. "Why don't you just go stay with your parents or something? You go there every time we have a break, anyway."

"Gee, I wonder why," I bit back.

"Oh, come on, you act like I'm a bad roommate," she scoffed.

"You are a bad roommate," I ground out. This was all so stupid and pointless. Why was I even engaging with her? My parents were missing, for the love of Christ!

Stacey jutted out her lip in a mutinous pout. "That's not true."

"You're standing in our room with all your friends trying to tell me who gets to stay in our room when I already told you 'no.' And you got beer and cum on my bed while I was gone—don't try to tell me you didn't," I snarled, my patience snapping. "Last time I checked, we're all nineteen/twenty years old. I don't mind you drinking, but if you get me in trouble for your bad choices, I will unleash holy hell on you, Stacey. And I've got better things to do than talk to you and your friends right now." I looked past her at Kelly and the rest of them. "Don't let the door hit you on the way out."

They all gaped at me as though no one had ever told them off before. Maybe they hadn't. But I was tired and confused, and I was scared for my parents, and my mouth just wasn't going to stay closed anymore.

"But... we voted," Kelly mumbled.

"Is this your room?" I asked.

"No," she replied.

"Your vote doesn't count. Now get out," I snarled.

I don't know what expression was on my face, but I've never seen a group of girls scatter so quickly.

Only Stacey stayed. She was white with rage. "This isn't over," she said.

"Bring it on, bitch," I growled.

She lifted her chin and stormed out the door.

I was actually kind of disappointed she didn't stick around for a physical fight. That thought alone told me I was way, way not myself.

Shaking with anger, I sat back down at my laptop, but I still couldn't get the numbers to make sense. With a frustrated sigh, I picked up my iPad and decided to go read out on the Northrup Mall.

When I left, I could see Stacey sneaking back into the room. Lord only knew what she was doing. Something deeply unpleasant or destructive for sure.

I decided not to circle back. I'd deal with whatever happened later. Just one more thing I could document to get myself moved to a different dorm room. I wished I could have kept my roommate from last year. Valerie was a real gem. But she'd unfortunately dropped out toward the end of the last semester, and I'd had to pay roommate roulette again.

I'd sure been shot in the face this time.

It was crisp and cool outside. I walked the few blocks to the

Northrup Mall quickly, enjoying the way the air burned just enough in my lungs to make me feel alive. Buses blared past as well as cars, but this was the one place in Minnesota where people walked across the street willy-nilly and no one questioned it. Pedestrians reigned supreme.

When I got to the mall, I could see all the trees were taken, but that was okay. On a cool day like this, I wanted to be in the sun, anyway. I sat down on the dying grass and started to read Shakespeare.

A long shadow fell over me.

"McKenzie Kent?" a deep voice asked.

I looked up...

... into the blue eyes of the most handsome man I'd ever seen in my life.

2
THUNDERSTRUCK

Will

It was a long shot, I knew, but after Caleb and Jacey rabbited on me before I could tell them who I was and why I'd sought them out, I'd had little choice but to dig deeper.

That put an even deeper dent into the finances I'd hidden from my grandfather, but it turned out, high-end jewelers were more than happy to take six-million-dollar cufflinks.

Three private investigators and some well-placed bribe money later, I was looking down at McKenzie Killeen. Or Kent, as it turned out. Maybe if I'd gone in with Kent, the Killeens wouldn't have run.

But that didn't matter now. What did matter was a head of long, thick, honey-colored hair and the most emerald green eyes I'd ever seen. She had a heart-shaped face, perfect, pouty lips….

Which she licked with the pink tip of her tongue.

I was a multi-billionaire bachelor. I'd seen that look before. Only I'd dressed down quite a bit, so I knew that look was lust for my body and not my money. She had no idea who the hell I was. I could use that.

"Yes?" she said breathily. Then she shook herself and cleared her throat. "Yes?" she repeated with more conviction.

Yes, please fuck me, Will. I gave her my best, sexiest, most inviting smile.

Her eyebrows drew together in confusion. "Sir?"

That shot me straight in the ego. I was eleven years her senior. I didn't let my smile falter, however. "I'm Will."

"Okay, Will…" she said with suspicion. "How did you know my name?"

Ah, yes. I had addressed her by name. The moment those green eyes met mine, I'd forgotten everything but my own name. "Sorry. I… do you mind if I sit down?"

McKenzie looked up and down the mall, probably to reassure herself that there were plenty of people around. There were. "It's a free mall," she shrugged.

I sank down into the grass, glad I'd worn jeans and a sweater rather than one of my suits. I'd even donned a pair of Hokas for the occasion instead of loafers. I regarded her for a moment. The intelligent spark in her eye and the set of her jaw told me she was a straight-shooter. I decided I'd better be as well, or she was going to rabbit on me, too. "I'm looking for your parents."

She frowned and clutched her iPad against her chest. Her thighs tensed as though preparing to spring up and run. "Are you the guy who came to our house?"

"Yes," I responded, my fingers twitching on my leg, ready to grab her if necessary. "But your parents didn't give me a chance to explain why I was there. They thought I was someone else. Or, rather, that I worked for someone they're afraid of. I don't. Frankly, I'm scared of him, too."

"Who?" she asked, and I gave her credit for not trying to run. Brave girl.

"Have you heard of William Masterson, Sr.?" I replied slowly. "He's my grandfather. He gave your parents a really hard time when they were younger. He also caused my father to kill himself. He's a very bad man, and I don't blame Caleb and Jacey at all for running, but I'm in trouble with my grandfather now, too, and I don't know what to do. I was hoping they could help me, but I scared them off."

McKenzie's lips thinned. "Yeah, you did. And I don't even think my uncles know where they went. I sure don't. I guess you're out of luck." She scrutinized me. "What did your grandfather do to my parents?"

"He trapped them, tried to kill them, made them do bad things for him... lots of stuff. Lots of bad, bad stuff. He's got a lot of money, you see, and he got most of it from doing illegal things. Bad things," I explained. "Your parents found out and testified against him. He's in prison, but he's still managing to do these bad things from there. I thought we were a legitimate company. I just found out about the rest. Now, my grandfather's after me because I'm not being a good little heir and helping him hurt people."

"I'm nineteen. Not nine. You can tell me what he did," she reminded me.

True. I took a deep breath. "Human trafficking, arms and drug dealing, stripping countries of their resources illegally... I think he might even be involved in the blood diamond trade, but I'm not sure. There was just so... much. I don't think I fully absorbed it all."

"And my parents found out about it?" she asked.

"Yes."

"And they testified against him, and he went to prison, and he's still managing to do all this *from* prison?" she rephrased.

"Yes," I said again.

"What do you think my parents can do about it?" she asked, confused.

"I... I honestly don't know. I don't know where else to turn," I admitted.

"How about the police?" she suggested.

I rubbed the back of my neck. "I tried. Every time I reach out to the authorities, I end up talking to someone who's being bribed by my grandfather. I'm actually on the run myself."

"Okay, so... the press?" she said.

"Tried that, too. I've been locked out of all my social media. I tried going to several papers and news stations, but my grandfather's always had someone there waiting for me. It's like he can see my every move," I sighed.

"And you thought it'd be a great idea to track down my parents and get them sucked into it, too?!" McKenzie protested.

I winced. "I didn't feel like I had another choice."

She rubbed her temples. "Okay. I'll call Uncle Jake. I'm sure he's the one who took care of everything before. He'll know what to do."

"Thank you. Do you want to use my phone?" I asked.

"You don't think your grandfather is tracking you through your phone?" she replied.

"I doubt it. It's a burner phone," I said.

McKenzie shook her head. "No. I'll call from a pay phone, just in case." She stood. "Well, are you coming?"

"Yes, ma'am," I teased her, and she blushed. Turnabout was fair play and all that.

We walked to a bar on Washington Avenue between the Northrup Mall and where I knew her dorm was. I stood to the side while she dialed a number, idly watching the news.

Feed of her farm home came up on the screen and I stared, watching as flames leapt high into the air. The building was clearly already beyond saving, even though the fire department was diligently hosing it down.

Three suspected dead in house fire, read the headline at the bottom.

McKenzie made a sound of consternation behind me. "He's not answer—"

I grabbed her arm and tried to yank her into my arms to shield her from seeing the three pictures that came up of her Uncle Jake, Uncle Billy, and Uncle Horace. But she struggled away from me.

"What do you think you're—oh my God." She stared up at the screen with wide, horrified eyes.

"I should never have tried to find your parents," I gritted out, hate for my grandfather boiling in my gut. It was his doing, I knew it.

She stood, shaking, staring at the screen.

I was trying to figure out what to do when two men in suits came into the college bar. They stood out like flamingos at a pigeon convention. "We need to go," I told her, grabbing her arm again.

"You... that... my..." she stuttered, still trying to wrap her head around what she was seeing.

I'd had a similar moment of complete shock not three weeks ago. While I understood, I also knew we were *both* in danger now. "McKenzie," I said, giving her a shake. "They're here for us."

She didn't seem to comprehend for a moment, and I wondered if I'd have to lift her over my shoulder and carry her out. But she finally saw the suited goons who were coming toward us. Turning pale, she spun around and bolted for the back door.

I was just glad there *was* a back door. I ran after her.

"Stay away from me!" she yelled when I came out the back door in her wake. "You're the reason all this is happening!"

"Yes," I admitted. "But now you're in danger because of me. We need to get out of here. I'm not going to let you face them alone."

"You just got done telling me your grandfather's keeping tabs on you no matter where you go! How does that help me?!" she shouted while we ran back toward the mall.

She had a point. I felt responsible for her now, though. I'd destroyed a nineteen-year-old's world because of my own desperation. "I have resources. We'll just—"

A state police squad car skidded to a stop next to the sidewalk just in front of us. The passenger window rolled down.

"Get in!" a voice rasped.

"Not on your life," I said and tried to grab McKenzie.

Much to my surprise, she went straight to the squad. "Uncle Jake!"

"Get in!" he repeated.

She launched herself into the back seat. I slid in after her. "He was talking to me, not you!" she snapped at me.

"No time." Jake pressed his foot down on the gas, and we sped over the Washington Avenue Bridge.

"Uncle Jake, it's this guy's fault. His name is—" she began.

"William Masterson III," he finished for her.

"Right. Will. He says people can track him anywhere," she continued. "He doesn't know how…"

"I would expect you've got a tracker under your skin, Mr. Masterson," Jake said.

Under my skin?! "Like a pet?!"

"Something like that, except more sophisticated. We'll stop somewhere, and I'll check." He stifled a groan.

"Uncle Jake, are you okay?" McKenzie asked.

"I will be, sweetheart." He pulled into a parking ramp, then turned to me. "Get out of the car and come to the driver's door. Right now."

Not knowing what else to do, and seeing as this was a cop, I got out of the car and went over to his door.

"Open it," he said.

"Oka-ay," I agreed and opened the door. What I saw made me freeze. "Sir, you're…"

The bloody, bullet-riddled man nodded. "Just kneel down. I have an idea where they might have put it."

I wanted to argue, but I didn't. I didn't think us getting found was going to get the officer much help. I knelt down.

He coughed, then moved bloody fingers along the base of my skull. He found a bump there I'd had all my life and nodded. "I thought so."

"That's not bone?" I asked.

"Not even a little bit." He reached a shaking hand in his pocket and took out a knife. "This isn't gonna tickle."

"Do it," I said flatly, grinding my teeth together against any cries of pain.

It hurt, him slicing me open, then digging around a bit. And I probably should have been more afraid he was going to sever my spinal cord or something. But right then, I was just too angry at my grandfather to think of anything but hate.

I heard his pocket knife click shut, and then his shaking hand held out a bloody electronic tag of some sort in front of my face.

"Step on that, won't you?" he asked.

"With pleasure," I responded. I dropped it on the concrete, then ground my heel into it. "I think it's best if we go now."

Jake nodded slowly. "I programmed a location into the burner phone in the cupholder there. You need to drive to it."

"Okay. So, let's…" I quickly held out my arms as he slumped sideways, barely catching him before he fell out of the car.

"You're going to be driving," he wheezed. "I'm just about dead. Someone will come to that location who can help you. Take care of McKenzie."

"Uncle Jake! *No!!!*" she screamed as he took one, last, rattling breath.

"Sweet J—" I stopped myself as a black sedan with dark, tinted windows came around the curve of the parking ramp. "We've got to go." I carefully lowered Jake's body to the concrete.

She was trying like hell to open her door, but it seemed he'd locked it before he died. "Uncle Jake!!!"

"McKenzie," I repeated. "We've got to go. They're here." I settled Jake's body away from the car and hopped in the driver's seat.

As I threw the car into gear and sped for the exit, she pressed her face to the back window.

"Uncle Jake!!!" she kept screaming. "Uncle Jake!!!"

3
THE ENEMY OF MY ENEMY

McKenzie

"We have to go back!" I beat the back of the driver's seat, causing Will to flinch. "We have to go back! He might be alive!"

"He's not," Will said.

"You don't know that!" I screamed, pummeling the cage.

He turned his head and gave me a sad, grim look. "I do know that."

The finality of it crushed my spirit. I slumped back in my seat and covered my face with my hands, crumpling in on myself. "Oh God."

"He was a good man," he said quietly. "I'm sure God will welcome him with open arms."

I glared at the back of his head through the cage. "Seriously? You're going to say that to me after all the damage you've caused?!"

Will sighed. "I'm sorry. You're right. I never should have come looking for your parents."

"Damn skippy you shouldn't have!" I yelled, but it came out as more of a croak.

"I can't change what I've done. But I will keep you safe." It wasn't so much a statement as a vow.

"You've been doing a bang-up job so far," I said nastily then regretted it. The man had just been looking for help. There was no way he could have known all this would happen. Or that he'd had a tracking device in him like a dog for who knew how long.

Could I honestly say, with a piece of work for a grandfather like his, I wouldn't have gone searching desperately for someone—anyone—to help me?

"I'm sorry, I shouldn't have said that. You're doing your best," I amended.

"Thanks, but I deserve whatever you have to throw at me," he replied. He glanced in the rearview mirror. "You can cry, you know. I won't judge."

Wasn't I crying? I touched my cheeks and realized that I wasn't. "I think I'm in too much shock. It hasn't hit me yet."

"Fair." He flicked his eyes back to the road.

Go past this light, then at the next one, turn left. Siri's voice was steady, calm. Even pleasant.

I wanted to chuck that bitch out the window, but we needed her to get to our destination. "I wonder who Uncle Jake is sending to help us?" I mused aloud.

"No clue. But it's got to be someone he really trusts." He took the left then looked back at me again. "I am really, truly sorry, McKenzie."

A lump formed in my throat, and I swallowed hard. "I mean, I'm not going to say it's okay, but I will say I understand. It's not your fault, Will. It's your grandfather's. I mean, what were you supposed to do? Be all happy about getting money from buying and selling people?"

"I should have figured out a way to handle things myself," he sighed. "I don't even know what I expected your parents to be able to do. I just know they went up against Goliath and won. I was hoping they could somehow help me do the same."

"If they'd let you talk to them, maybe things might have turned out differently. Who knows?" I shrugged. "We're just stuck now, I guess."

"I guess so," he agreed.

We fell into an awkward silence, Siri the only voice breaking it from time to time.

In fifty-three miles, turn left...

And then Siri went silent for a while. I didn't expect we'd hear her again until two miles to the left turn.

The sun set. Streetlights became fewer and further between. In the dim light of the moon, when there weren't oncoming headlights—and soon there were very few of those as well—I saw corn fields turn into forest. Without streetlights, the woods seemed to press in on us.

In two miles, turn left... Siri said.

"She's just too damn cheerful," Will muttered.

"I know, right?" I responded, hunching my shoulders. "Isn't there a funeral Siri?"

"Maybe hearses get her." He tapped the glowing screen, clearly trying to find some less chirpy setting for Siri.

I laughed. Then I felt bad for laughing. Uncle Jake was dead. Still, the laughter kept rolling out of me until I was holding my sides and hysterical. Tears rolled down my cheeks, and I sobbed and laughed at the same time. It was super weird.

He took the left turn, and then we were on a dirt road. Not gravel. Dirt. The squad bumped over tree roots, rocks, and uneven patches. "We're almost there," he said. "I think it's at the end of this... whatever this is. Road? Driveway?"

"O-Okay," I managed to choke out.

Will and I stopped at a destination where there wasn't a building in sight. In fact, it seemed as though we were just at some random place in the middle of the woods. "Okay," he said. "I sort of thought we were going to a cabin or something..." He opened his door and the dome light came on. He looked at me in the rearview mirror, then got out and opened the back door.

"Hey." He slid in next to me and put a hand on my arm. "We're going to get through this."

I hiccuped and kept laughing/crying.

Much to my surprise, he inched closer and opened his arms, inviting me in.

I really didn't know what else to do to make myself calm down. I leaned into Will, and his arms closed around me, holding me tight.

"I'm not going to tell you it's going to be okay because I don't want to lie to you," he said softly, his breath ruffling my hair. "But we are going to get through this. We're both smart, capable adults. And as far as we know, your parents are okay. There's a lot of reason to hope."

"Uncle Jake is dead," I rasped. "And probably Uncle Billy and Uncle Horace, too." My tears soaked into his sweater. It felt soft against my cheek. Cashmere? *Why the fuck am I worried about what his sweater is made out of right now?!* I berated myself. Still, there was something comforting about it, like a nice, warm security blanket. Or maybe it was the man in the sweater. He smelled like days spent lying out by the pool and nights drinking fine cognac. There was just something very solid and relaxed about him.

My breathing evened out, and I stopped my gasping, hiccuping giggles.

Will rubbed my arms with his hands. "That's better."

I did feel better. And felt bad for feeling better. But me losing my cool right now wasn't going to help anybody. "Are we supposed to wait here for Uncle Jake's contact, do you think?" I asked, turning my attention back to the situation at hand.

"Let me check the phone." He held onto me a beat longer than necessary, and I could have sworn he breathed in the scent of my hair. But he let go before I could be sure and went back to the front seat, taking the phone out of the cupholder. "I'm not... oh. There's a text from an unknown number. It says we're supposed to switch cars here."

"Switch... to what? I don't see a car," I said, scooting out of the back seat. My shoes crunched on dead leaves.

He jumped then relaxed when he saw it was just me. "Maybe it's under a tarp or something. Here." He turned on the phone's flashlight and began pointing it around.

Sure enough, not five yards ahead of us, there was a cammo tarp off to the side of the path. He turned off the squad and pocketed the keys then guided us to the tarp.

Together, we pulled it off a nondescript silver Camry with Wisconsin plates.

There was a low ding, and he looked down at the phone screen. "Another text. Says keys are above the visor."

"I hope the tires are still good," I said with trepidation, wondering how long the Camry might have been parked out here in the middle of nowhere.

"Only one way to find out." He opened the driver's door and flipped down the visor. A key fell into his hand.

"We'd better hope the battery's still working, too," I added. I went around the side of the car and got into the passenger seat. I wasn't going to fight over who got to drive. I was barely out of an attack of hysterics. Will seemed to be the most solid one of the two of us right now. Our best bet was for him to drive.

He got in behind the wheel then frowned at the phone. "It says ditch this phone."

"What? How are we going to know where we're going?" I asked.

"Check the glove compartment," he said, and I knew he was quoting the text word for word.

I opened the glove compartment and took out a paper map. The kind that folded. I'd never seen one in my entire life. "Uh…"

"Is there something marked on it?" he asked, leaning over as I unfolded the map.

Sure enough, there was red marker highlighting a route into Iowa. "Yeah, someone traced a route."

"Good." He tossed the phone then shut the driver's door. "Buckle up."

I did, just as headlights shone down the road behind the squad car. "Um… Will? I think—"

"I think we need to get out of here," he agreed without even catching the end of my sentence. He started the car and pulled out onto the dirt path.

The Camry bumped along violently as we followed the road the other way. I hoped it came out on a street and that we weren't going to be cornered, but it wasn't like we could go back the other way.

Mercifully, the dirt path led us straight to blacktopped road.

"All right, navigator, which way are we going?" he asked.

I admired his even, patient tone. I was freaking out. "Um..." I looked down at the map. I was a sophomore in college. I could do this. "Left. No! Right. Which way is Highway 35 South?"

"Left." He turned, and we started down the road.

I glanced at the speedometer. "You're not going very fast."

"I'm going the speed limit. If we get pulled over, then we're done," he pointed out.

Oh. "Oh, right."

Headlights showed up behind us, and someone began speeding up our tail. "Shit," Will said, looking in the rearview mirror.

"Is it the people from the woods?" I asked anxiously.

"I don't know for sure, but it'd be quite a coincidence if it wasn't. We're the only two cars on this stretch of road, as far as I can tell," he grunted.

As the car behind us got closer, I saw that it had bars in front. "I think they're going to ram us."

"I think so, too," he said.

"What do we do?" I asked, looking at Will.

He set his jaw. "We go faster." And he stomped his foot down on the accelerator.

4
BUMPER CARS

Will

We weren't going to be able to out-run these guys. There wasn't a snowball's chance in Hades. Yet, as I put my foot to the floor, damned if the Camry didn't lurch forward with the force of a muscle car. "What the hell?" I muttered.

"I think we've got something under the hood that's not the factory motor," McKenzie said, clutching the handle above her head. "Sorry, it's not that I don't trust you, it's just that we're going really fast, and I grabbed the 'oh-shit' bar on instinct."

I blinked. "'Oh-shit bar'?"

"Yeah. This thing. Why, what do you call it?" she asked.

Despite our situation, I had to laugh. "I don't think I've ever called it anything, but thanks for letting me know what it's called. I'll bet that's exactly what they call it on the factory floor, too."

"They might. You never know," she replied defensively.

There was a slam, and the car jerked, wrenching at our bodies as the car behind us rammed us. It took every bit of driving knowledge I had—and I had a fair bit from a penchant for driving fast cars—to keep us on the road.

"We can't get caught," McKenzie told me. "Do whatever it takes."

"Noted. Hang on tight." I hadn't been considering the maneuver with a passenger in the car, but since I had her blessing, I went for it. Like she said, we couldn't get caught.

I spun the wheel, and suddenly, we were facing the bastards.

"What are you doing?!" she shouted.

"Hang on to your panties," I responded and maneuvered around the other car. When they turned to give chase, I jerked the wheel again and knocked them at an angle.

Then I slammed on the brakes, even pulling the emergency brake to keep us out of the other car's orbit, as our pursuer fishtailed, then skidded off the road and wrapped around a tree.

"Did... did we just kill somebody?" McKenzie asked in the silence that followed.

I pushed the emergency brake back into place and turned the car, heading down the road once more. "I'm trying not to think about it." That was a lie. It was all I could think about. But we needed to put distance between us and the might-be-dead pursuer(s) before the police showed up.

My knuckles turned white as I gripped the steering wheel, trying to keep my mind on the path ahead.

She put a hand on my thigh. "It's okay. You had no choice. They would have hurt us."

"McKenzie, do me a favor?" I asked.

"Yeah? What?" she replied.

"I want you to slap me really, really hard if I ever start thinking killing people is 'okay,'" I said.

She pulled her hand away and nodded. "I can do that."

"Good."

* * *

Hours later, I glanced down and saw our new problem. "We're running low on gas."

McKenzie, to her credit, had stayed alert, if mostly silent, the entire time we'd been driving. She glanced up from the map spread across her lap. "I have my wallet."

"I do, too. We have to remember only to use cash. I'm more concerned about cameras, actually, but we should both make a pit stop," I said.

"You're just like Uncle Billy. Nobody needs to pee until we need gas," she chuckled.

I winced. "You could have told me you needed to go."

"I'm just teasing you. I guess. Sorry. I'm fine. But yeah, it's always a good idea to empty the tank when you fill the tank. Cuts down on stops. And cameras," she agreed.

"We'll pick up a couple of baseball caps," I suggested. "Then we won't have to worry as much about it."

"Good idea." She blinked up at the bright overhead lights as we pulled off the highway and into a gas station right off the exit. "Probably a good idea to get some food or something while we're here, too. I mean, not that I'm hungry. Just that we're going to need it eventually."

I nodded. "Yes, that is also a good idea. We can both shop for stuff together. It's not as though we know each other's likes and dislikes yet."

McKenzie giggled. "'As though.' It's a gas station. They won't have caviar."

"Pardon me for having a stuffy education." I grinned. "Anyway, here we are. We'll both go in together."

"I don't suppose it would help if we went in together, like, *together* together," she said.

I raised an eyebrow. "To fool the cameras, I'm assuming?"

She blushed a brilliant red. "Yeah, to fool the cameras! What else?"

"So many possibilities," I murmured, then stopped myself. Aside from a flicker of interest at first seeing me, she hadn't been eyeing me like steak. Not like I was eyeing her. I tried to remind myself that I was thirty, and she was nineteen, but the angel on my shoulder seemed to be vacationing while the devil on the other side was salivating. She was chesty with a nice, round ass. Just the way I liked my women. But she also had strength and intelligence, and that was damned sexy, too.

"Oh, get your head out of the gutter." She smacked my arm, breaking my concentration. My concentration that had been concentrated right on her breasts. "It's just for show. I mean, you're hot and all, but we're in a situation."

I shook myself. "Right. Right. Sorry. You are also 'hot and all,' by the way."

McKenzie blushed again, and I thanked my lucky stars I wasn't a schoolboy anymore and didn't get flushed so easily, or I would have been blushing, too. "Then it shouldn't be any hardship to put your arm around me in the store."

"No hardship at all." My voice was gravelly.

She swatted me again and then got out of the car.

I got out as well and came around the car just as she was closing her door. I slid an arm around her shoulders and tucked her into my side. Damned if her soft curves didn't fit perfectly there. My dick perked up, hopeful little fucker. I had to tell it very sternly that there was no hope here. As she said, we were in a 'situation.' There were more important things to be thinking about than dragging McKenzie into the men's room and screwing her until we were both completely senseless.

We picked up a basket at the door then went to the counter. I pulled out my money clip and she made a surprised sound. Maybe I should have been keeping fewer hundreds in my money clip.

The cashier's eyes bulged. "How can I help you, sir?"

"Gas on number five," I said. "And we'll be doing a little shopping in here. Do you happen to have baseball caps? We like to drive with the windows down, but it's been doing a real number on my angel's hair."

"Absolutely, sir. There's a rack right over there." He pointed.

I laid a hundred on the counter. "After we're done with the gas, you can keep the change. Consider it a tip."

McKenzie made a disapproving sound in her throat but didn't comment until the cashier had happily put the hundred in the till.

"What?" I asked as we walked over to the hats.

"Normal people don't give fifty-dollar tips to gas station attendants," she mumbled.

"They should. Working man deserves to be paid what he's worth," I said.

"Yes, but we're trying to keep a low profile," she reminded me.

Oh, right. She had a point. "I'll… be better next time."

She picked up some hats praising Minnesota then laughed at one and put it on my head. "Minnesota state bird."

I plucked it off my head, looked at it, and let out a chuckle. "The mosquito. Isn't that the truth."

"Now, let's see here. I need one, too." She perused the selection.

"Found one!" I grabbed a purple hat with two demons shivering on it.

McKenzie took it and frowned at the words. "The Vikings won the Super Bowl?"

"Yes. You know, hell froze over? Get it?" I asked.

"Are you a Packers fan?" she accused me.

"Sadly, no. Skol!" I smiled.

She laughed then handed the hat back to me. "Okay. I'll wear it. I got to pick yours, after all."

I adjusted the back strap, then plopped it on her head. "There. Now we're all ready to go."

"Except for groceries," she reminded me.

"Right. Bathroom first, though. At least for me." We broke apart and headed to the facilities, setting the empty basket on a nearby shelf to return to.

Once we got out, we found out very quickly that we had very similar tastes in food. Almost identical, in fact. The only thing I threw in the basket that she didn't like was Funyuns. The only thing she threw in that I didn't like was dark chocolate with a hint of chili from Lindt.

"I can't believe you eat that stuff," we said together.

"Jinx, you owe me a pop," she inserted quickly.

"Pick one out," I chuckled.

"You're not supposed to talk until you buy me the pop," she explained. "That's how it works."

I made a zipping motion across my lips but had to stifle a laugh when she grabbed a Dr. Pepper.

"What's so funny?" she asked.

I leaned over her to grab a Dr. Pepper of my own.

We were still smiling when we got to the register. The cashier winked at us. "You two are a cute couple."

"Thanks," I said and she pinched me.

"You broke the jinx again!" she complained.

I laid another hundred on the counter, which the cashier happily put in the till. "No change. Thank you."

McKenzie rolled her eyes. She started to grab the plastic bags of our food, but I snatched them up before she could. "A gentleman doesn't let his woman do the heavy lifting," I teased.

She blushed again and I saw the same flicker of desire in her eyes I'd seen when she first looked up at me at the U of M. "That's kind of sexist."

"I think you mean to say, 'That's kind of sexy,'" I corrected her, then bumped her hip with mine.

"Ugh. Men." She stomped toward the door.

I had to get an eyeful of the way her jeans perfectly molded themselves around her beautiful bottom. I couldn't help myself. My dick perked up again.

"Dude, you are one lucky sonofabitch," the cashier said, leaning over the counter to get a look as well.

Part of me wanted to punch him for ogling what was mine. But it would have been like punching him for admiring the Venus de Milo. And she wasn't mine. At least, not yet. "Tell me about it," I murmured.

McKenzie looked back over her shoulder. "Are you coming or not?"

My dick interpreted her words in its own special way, and I had to start thinking of anything else. "Sure am." I followed her out.

She arranged the food in the back seat within easy reach, putting a Dr. Pepper in each of our cupholders while I pumped the gas.

Watching her breasts jiggle in her shirt while she got everything set up the way she wanted did nothing for my problem.

"McKenzie?" I asked, squeezing a few more drops of fuel into the tank after it had clicked to stop initially.

"Hmm?" she responded.

"When we've resolved this 'situation,' I'd like to take you out for a steak dinner," I said.

She looked up. "Really?"

"I can't think of anything I'd like to do more than that," I confessed.

McKenzie then smiled at me, and it was a sunbeam straight to my heart. "I'd like that, too," she said.

5
ANOTHER FARM

McKenzie
Even though it was night, I still looked out the window often to see what there was to see in the moonlight. As we neared Iowa and went into the state itself, all there was to see were farms on flat land.

Lots of farms. Lots of flat land.

"Scenery's not going to change," Will said after a while. "You can take a nap, if you want. It looks like we're driving straight to Des Moines. That's going to take hours."

"I don't need a nap. I don't think I could take one even if I wanted to," I admitted. "Today's been…"

"Insane," he finished for me.

"Insane," I echoed. "That's the understatement of the century. Jake died. We're being chased by your grandfather's people—"

"We think," he interrupted.

I turned and stared at him. "We think? What do you mean, 'we think'?"

"My grandfather wasn't the only person looking for your parents. They're poised to testify against a sheik, if Interpol ever finds him, and also I think something called the Trinary. A group of assassins, as far as I can tell. They were hunting your parents for the ransom," he said.

"Ransom?" I repeated. "What ransom?"

"I'm not sure if it's being offered anymore or not, honestly. My grandfather went to prison, and the sheik is on the run, so, whatever capturing your parents was going to do has gone to pot." He sighed. "I wish I understood more of what's going on, but I barely got out of the office as it was."

I frowned at him. "How did you, of all people, find my parents when this sheik and your grandfather couldn't?"

Will glanced at me, then swallowed. "My grandfather had the information already. Or, rather, he had the name of the police officer who was helping your parents—Jake. I just took that information, gave it to a private investigator, and he must have followed Jake to your Uncle Billy's farm. Or something. I'm not sure why my grandfather didn't do that himself years ago. Maybe he thought he had enough information to find them if he wanted to."

"So, my parents were never really safe," I murmured.

"No. I don't think they were. I'm surprised they managed to stay out of my grandfather's crosshairs for thirty years. It's not like Grandfather to leave loose ends," he said.

"How long is your grandfather in for?" I asked.

"He gets out at the end of this year. He would have been out five years ago, but apparently, they caught him doing something." He shrugged. "I have no idea what. You'd think if they'd caught him doing the human trafficking, they would have tacked on another twenty-five years."

I looked down at the map, my eyes swimming with angry tears. "Your grandfather's a real do-it-yourself-er, isn't he?"

"Yes. How did you know?" he asked.

"I think your grandfather's known exactly where my parents are for the last thirty years. But I think he was planning on punishing them as soon as he got out," I said. "Himself."

Will stared out at the road. "I think you're right."

"You only moved the timeline forward. This was always going to happen," I whispered. "Hell, I'll bet you saved my parents' lives. I just wish Uncle Billy, Uncle Horace, and Uncle Jake had run, too."

"I still feel like it's my fault they're dead," he said quietly. He slammed his palm on the steering wheel. "Damn it!"

I put my hand on his thigh, and some of the tension left him, though a muscle still twitched along his jawline. "I mean it. You saved my parents. You probably saved me. I'll bet your grandfather would have had a great time dangling me over my parents' heads."

"He would have," he agreed. "I guess I screwed up his plans in more ways than one."

"What do you mean by that?" I asked.

"He ultimately wanted me to take over the family business, I think. *All* of the family businesses. I guess he thought my moral compass would point more in his direction if he raised me right. Joke's on him. I turned out more like my father, or so I'm told," he said.

"Your father must be a good man." I frowned as his expression turned sad.

"I think he was. I never met him. My grandfather drove him to kill himself, which I also found out recently," he whispered.

Oh God. I patted his thigh sympathetically. "I'm sorry."

"Me, too."

We both stared out at the road for at least an hour. I didn't take my hand off his thigh. I wanted him to know I was there for him, as he seemed wrapped up in some pretty dark thoughts.

"Want a beef jerky?" he finally asked, breaking the silence so abruptly that it made me jump.

"Please don't tell me that's some kind of innuendo," I said.

Will laughed, and the tension eased. "No. I really mean beef jerky. I think if you did anything about 'innuendo' right now, I'd drive off the road."

"I'm holding out for that steak dinner," I teased. "I don't want you to think I'm easy."

He laughed harder. "Right. Because I am completely convinced I could buy you with just a steak dinner."

I stopped as I was reaching into the back seat for the food. "Hey now. Don't think I can be bought at any price."

"Not even a diamond tennis bracelet?" he asked.

I knew he was kidding, but some small part of me was still offended. "Will, I know you come from a different world than I do. But in my world, I'm not interested in your money. I'm interested in you."

He looked over at me with the most heartbreaking expression I'd ever seen. Something like longing, sadness, and desperation all rolled into one. "You really mean that?"

I smacked his arm. "Of course I do, idiot! Jeez, what kind of people do you hang out with?"

"Not very good ones, as it turns out," he muttered.

It occurred to me that he was probably more often evaluated by his wallet than by his character by other women who traveled in his circle. The thought depressed me on his behalf. "Beef jerky?" I asked, unwrapping one and holding it out to him.

Will took it and gnawed on it, his face unreadable. "You know I'm thirty, and you're nineteen, right?"

"Right," I replied. "Age is just a number. And guys my age? They have the maturity of a tadpole. I think they only think about their tadpoles."

He chuckled. "As a man, I can tell you it doesn't get that much better as we age. We just hide it better."

"Liar," I said.

"No, trust me. I've been thinking about my tadpoles since the moment I met you," he responded.

"Not the whole time, though," I corrected him.

Will glanced over at me again. "It's at least been on the back burner."

"I mean, I could say the same thing. Like I said, you're hot." I didn't mind telling him this. I'd told him before, and we were thrown together in this situation, anyway. It wasn't as though I had a girlfriend to gush to. Or my mother. Besides, he and I might as well be honest with each other. We might be together... God only knew how long.

"You are not doing anything to stop me thinking about tadpoles," he chuckled.

I shrugged. "I figure it's better to be straightforward. Who knows how long it'll be until we get to have that steak dinner?"

"You're saying you think we're going to sleep together before I even get to treat you to a steak dinner?" He blinked.

"I don't know. We don't know how this is going to go. But I do think we're going to be seeing a lot of each other for a while, and I just wanted you to know I was open to the idea," I said.

He let out a long breath. "I never thought having such a frank conversation was going to leave me in need of a cold shower."

I grinned. "I guess it is kind of hot in here now."

Will groaned and picked up my Dr. Pepper, shaking it gently in my face. "You need to drink this and not talk for a bit. I am *this* close to begging you for things we shouldn't be doing in a moving vehicle. And I haven't even kissed you yet."

"You like to do things in their proper order. I get it." I felt bold taking the Dr. Pepper and swigging it. In truth, I was pretty inexperienced with guys. A very disappointing high school sweetheart experience was the only notch I had on my bedpost.

He took his Dr. Pepper and drank it as well.

We fell into a companionable silence. Then Des Moines loomed in front of us.

"Does it say where in the city we're supposed to go?" he asked.

I looked back down at the map. "The line passes through and goes a little west. We have to turn right on Highway Six. We're going somewhere called Adel."

"And after that?" he prodded. "Is there a hotel or house or address or something?"

I flipped the map back and forth. "Umm..." Then I saw the list of cities. Next to Adel was an address in red pen. "Yes." I rattled it off to him.

"We'll have to ask at a gas station or something where that address is. They're going to look at us like we're nuts for not having a phone or some kind of navigation," he sighed. "Oh well. Can't be helped."

Highway 6 came into sight, and I pointed. "Right here."

Will nodded and took a right. Soon, we were back out in farm country.

"Sign says we should be in Adel in about twenty-five miles," he said after a few minutes.

"So, twenty-five-ish minutes," I interpreted.

"We are definitely from Minnesota." He shook his head. "We're going to have to work on that."

"Oh. Yeah, true. I guess we don't usually talk about things in terms of miles," I conceded.

"It's Minnesota. Miles isn't going to tell you anything. Have you ever been on 494 during rush hour?" he asked.

I shuddered. "God, don't remind me."

"Exactly."

We continued into the cute, historic Adel. Will found a gas station, and we stopped at a pump. "Might as well get more gas. This thing gets great gas mileage, I've got to say."

"It's a Toyota," I said. "Should we get more Dr. Pepper, too?"

"Is that really a question?" he grinned.

"No, not really," I smiled back.

We walked into the gas station, pulling our baseball caps low on our foreheads. "Hi," I said, going right to the counter. "We'd like to buy gas. Also, we're a little lost. Do you know where this address is?" I pointed to the address scribbled on the map.

Will lay down a hundred, then two, then three, all the way up to a thousand dollars. "And we'd like you to forget we were here."

"You got it," the cashier said. He took out his phone and brought up the address. "That's a vacation rental, I think. It's listed on VRBO, anyway. But here's the directions." He pulled them up and showed them to Will.

Will looked them over and nodded. "Okay. Thank you very much." He laid down another hundred. "That's for the gas. Keep the change. Oh, and two Dr. Peppers."

"Knock yourself out, friend," the cashier replied, pocketing the money. "You can rob the store now for all I care."

"Maybe on our next vacation," he said with a slight smile.

We grabbed our Dr. Peppers, fueled up the Camry, and headed for the vacation home.

"If we get there, and it's full of your grandfather's people, I am going to be super pissed off," I told him.

"If we get there and it's full of my grandfather's people, we're making a run for it," he responded. "Because I'm not letting him get his hands on you."

"What if we get trapped?" I asked.

He rested a hand on my shoulder. "If we get trapped, then I will do everything in my power to get you out."

I took his hand and squeezed it. "Just so you know, despite everything, it's been really nice getting to know you, Will Masterson III."

"Likewise, McKenzie Kent," he replied softly.

6
JAKE'S FRIEND

Will

I drove down a nondescript driveway to a nondescript house. Apparently, its location near the historic parts of Adel was much more of a draw than the house itself, because for a VRBO, it looked rather drab. Not that I'd ever stayed in a VRBO. Or anything with less than a five-star rating, for that matter.

"This place is kind of boring for a VRBO," McKenzie remarked, confirming my suspicions.

"Maybe that's a good thing? My grandfather would certainly never look for me in a place like this. Not to sound snooty," I added the last part quickly.

She shrugged. "Different strokes for different folks. You've just had a different upbringing than most people, that's all. And if it means your grandfather won't look for you here, all the better."

"Right," I said. I parked the Camry in front of the garage. A detached garage.

We both looked up at the house proper. I imagined McKenzie was feeling the same trepidation I was and reached for her hand.

She threaded her fingers through mine, and we sat there for a while, just staring at the house, contemplating what the future might hold.

"I suppose we should just get it over with," she finally sighed.

I nodded, but neither of us moved, even to take our seat belts off.

The side door, just next to the detached garage, banged open, and we both jumped, revealing a grizzled old man with a wild, kinky beard and bushy eyebrows. The most notable thing about him, however, was the shotgun in his hand.

"Tarnation!" he yelled. "Are you comin' in or not?!"

McKenzie swallowed and withdrew her hand from mine so she could unbuckle her seat belt. "I guess that's our invitation."

"I figure we'd better go inside," I agreed, unclicking my own seat belt.

We got out of the car and started toward the old man.

He put his shotgun to his shoulder, and I grabbed McKenzie's wrist and pulled her behind me.

Then the old man lowered the shotgun. "Hmph. Squirrel. Damn vermin makin' trouble all the time. Can't hardly tell if there's a real threat comin' or not." He turned and motioned for us to follow him into the house.

I wasn't sure it was a good idea to throw our lot in with Mr. Trigger-Happy, but it wasn't like we had much of a choice. I glanced at McKenzie, who'd come out from behind me.

"We might as well follow him in," she said, her voice tight.

Was she angry with me? "Yes. Might as well." I reached for her hand again, but she tugged it away.

Frowning, I decided to let her have her space. Clearly, I'd done something to upset her. I just didn't know what that was. Besides, we had a gun-toting mountain man to worry about. I decided I'd ask her about it when we were in a safer position.

The old man waited inside the door, tapping his foot impatiently. We hurried into the house. He shut and locked the door. It had three different bolts. Two of them looked brand new. "Took you long enough," the old man grumped. "You know them Camrys can go six-hundred-and-ten miles before they need more gas. You must've stopped at least twice when you didn't have to."

"We needed food. And, you know, other things," I said defensively.

"Y'all could've pissed in a bottle," he replied.

McKenzie and I both made a face. "I suppose I could have," I explained. "But... well... women..."

"We don't have the whole aim thing going for us." She rescued me from my awkward stuttering.

"Hmph." The old man's eyes narrowed on us. "Soft. Y'all are too soft. Dunno how I'm gonna keep you alive and outta trouble."

"We appreciate anything you can do," I said while McKenzie nodded along with my statement.

"And you're too hifalutin'." The old man shook his head. "Well, I gotta work with what I got, I guess. My name's Lyle. But my friends call me Hoot."

I bit down hard on my lip. I was not going to laugh. I was *not* going to laugh.

"'Hoot'?" she echoed.

Hoot nodded. "Long story. We ain't got time for it. I already loaded up the Suburban. You're gonna park the Camry in the garage after I pull 'er out."

"Okay," I said. "I can do that."

"Maybe let me do something," she grumbled.

I turned to her. "What?"

"No fightin'. We ain't got time for that, either." Hoot went to the kitchen table and pulled back the tablecloth, revealing two identical handguns. "Y'all need to grab one of these. And don't be puttin' it down the front of your pants, Mr. Bigshot. You'll blow your dick off."

"I'm not... sure we're... comfortable with guns..." I said.

McKenzie rolled her eyes. "I am. Uncle Jake taught me how to use one." Her expression grew sad. "Uncle Jake died, Hoot."

Hoot hissed, then drew himself up and squared his shoulders. "Happens to the best of us. All right, grab the guns and let's go."

McKenzie took one of the guns and shoved it in the waistband of her jeans at her back. I followed suit, hoping I'd never have occasion to use the thing.

We walked out of the house, and I moved the Camry while she looked on with a frown on her face. Oh yes. We were definitely having a talk soon.

Hoot pulled a black Suburban out of the garage. I was surprised the beast had fit in there. "You go on and park 'er inside."

I parked the Camry. She headed for the passenger seat.

"Not a chance," Hoot said. "Y'all need to be able to duck down in the back. Back seat, both of you."

She let out a huff of frustration and wrenched the door open. I calmly held it for her so it didn't swing back in and hit her in the ass. Then I got in next to her.

"Buckle up, if that's your thing." Hoot started down the road.

I buckled up. She didn't.

"Please don't let whatever this is going on between us compromise your safety," I said to her.

Grumbling under her breath, she buckled her seat belt.

"Thank you." I turned as much as my seat belt would allow me to and faced her. "Now, will you please tell me what I did wrong?"

"You don't need to get all protective," she responded. "I could have handled myself."

"Handled yourself when?" I asked, confused.

"When Hoot was pointing the shotgun at us," she replied.

I blinked at her. "You could have handled yourself as in you could have stopped a bullet?"

McKenzie folded her arms over her chest. "No, but I could have taken one as well as you could have."

"I didn't want you to take a bullet," I said. "I wanted me to take a bullet and you to run."

"What if I wanted to take a bullet and for you to run?" she argued. "You're not going to pull the man card on me, are you?"

I folded my arms over my chest as well. "Maybe I am."

"Ugh. I hate it when men pull the man card," she grunted. "It's very sexist."

"I'm not going to apologize for wanting to keep you alive," I replied.

"You've got a lot of piss and vinegar in you, little missy," Hoot called from the front. "But my job is to keep *you* alive. Mr. Prissy Pants is just a close second. So if you get a gun pointed at you, yeah, let the big bastard get between you and a bullet."

She grinned and I felt the tension ease. "'Mr. Prissy Pants'?"

"My name is Will," I muttered, glaring at Hoot in the rearview mirror.

"I know. William Masterson *the Third*. Like that ain't the most prissy pants name on the planet," Hoot snorted.

"It is kind of prissy," she agreed.

I gave her my best puppy-dog pout. "Whose side are you on?"

"Hoot's, of course," she laughed.

"Good side to be on, too," Hoot said.

I sighed. "I guess I can't win."

"It ain't about winning, kid. It's about living," Hoot informed me with an air of folkish wisdom.

"Can't argue with that," she said. "I, for one, would like to live."

"So, then why are you mad about me wanting to take a bullet for you?" I asked.

"It's the principle of the thing," she sniffed. Then she gave in with a sigh. "Okay, it was kind of heroic."

"Thank you," I replied. "I thought so, too."

"Don't get a big head about it. It was only kind of heroic." But her mischievous smile belied her words.

I grinned back. "Well, Hoot's decided I can take all your bullets for you, so I suppose we won't be arguing in the future?"

"Not about this, I guess," she said.

"Yeah, you got to be careful about women, son. You never know when an argument's comin'," Hoot cautioned me.

"Gee, thanks, Hoot," she sighed. "Ugh. Misogyny lives."

"You've been takin' too many of them Women's Studies classes at the U," Hoot decided.

I was now trying very hard not to laugh as her scowl zeroed in on

Hoot instead of me. "You mean Gender, Women & Sexuality Studies?" she responded archly.

"Yeah. Them studies," he said. "They done gone and fried your brain."

"I suppose a woman's place is in the kitchen, too?" she growled.

He winked at me in the rearview mirror. "I can think of a few other places. Way he's been lookin' at you, I think he's thought of a few, too."

"Oh my God. Let me out. I'll walk," she groaned.

I patted her shoulder. "I think you're brilliant. Don't mind Hoot. I think he's trying to get you riled up on purpose."

"You're probably right." She leaned her head on my shoulder and every thought I'd ever had suddenly flew from my mind as my blood started pooling southward. "Hoot, do you suppose we can get some sleep now?"

"I don't want you knowin' where we're goin', so I figure now's the best time," he replied. "You two get some shut-eye. I'll let you know when we stop for gas."

"Okay. Because if you make me pee in a bottle, I will be extremely pissed off," she yawned.

Hoot grinned. "And let you ruin my seats? That ain't gonna happen."

"Good." She closed her eyes and snuggled into my shoulder.

"You ain't gonna be sleepin', are you?" he asked after her breathing evened out.

"I would, but certain anatomy is making it difficult," I replied. I traced my fingers over McKenzie's hairline, brushing a stray lock of honey-colored hair off her face.

"Heh-heh. That's a prissy way of sayin' you got a hard-on," he chuckled.

My cheeks flushed. "Yes, well, it's going to be a long ride to wherever we're going if this is all it takes."

"True. But you wouldn't be a young man if a pretty girl like McKenzie didn't get you goin'." He glanced at me. "If you break her heart, I'll break every bone in your body. It's the least I can do for Jack."

"If I break her heart, I *want* you to break every bone in my body," I responded.

Hoot nodded. "Good to know we're on the same page."

I looked down at her again. McKenzie took my breath away the way no other woman ever had.

My heart did a little flip-flop, and I knew then that I was in big, big trouble.

7
TEXAS BOUND

McKenzie

I woke up with Will's head leaning on top of mine. He was breathing deeply, his arm draped around my shoulders. The way he sat was protective. It was endearing. And annoying. And endearing.

"Shh, don't wake him up," Hoot whispered. "He finally fell asleep."

"Okay," I whispered back. I wondered what had stopped him from falling asleep earlier.

Hoot chuckled softly, and I decided there must be some inside joke I wasn't getting. "Still got a lotta hours to go."

"Where are we going?" I asked.

"Texas," he said simply.

"Where in Texas?" I glanced up to see there was a map resting on the dashboard.

He flipped it over. "Never you mind. If we get caught, best you don't know."

"Okay." I focused my attention elsewhere. Elsewhere happened to be Will's chest and abs. He was wearing a sweater, and it fit him well, but it still didn't hide the fact that he was built. I wondered how much time he spent at the gym. I wondered how it would feel to touch abs as muscular as I imagined his were.

I licked my lips. I was in trouble for sure. I'd basically told him to go ahead and jump me after steak, before steak, independent of steak…. What had I been thinking?!

Of course, I wanted to climb him like one of those rock walls at REI, but that was beside the point. I should probably have played a *little* hard to get.

Everything that was a feminist in me balked at that idea. I'd done the grown up, womanly thing and told Will I thought he was hot. He'd said the same about me. It was better that way than batting my eyelashes and fiddling with my keys or whatever it was women did to be coy. Coy wasn't really in my wheelhouse.

"What are you thinking about so hard?" Will yawned, blinking down at me as he woke up.

"You're supposed to be sleeping, mister. Hoot told me you just fell asleep," I admonished him.

He shrugged, and it made my head, which was still resting on his shoulder, bob. "I guess I'm not that tired."

"You're a poor liar, son," Hoot said. "You're just havin' a situation in the southerly department and don't wanna tell McKenzie about it."

"And thank you for that," Will sighed.

"I guess it's good I'm not a guy," I grinned.

"Right now? Yes. Very good." Will shifted in his seat, and I realized he wasn't kidding about his problem. "I could still smell your hair while I was sleeping. I was either about to have a very good dream or I needed to wake myself up."

I frowned, confused. "Why not just have a good dream?"

"Because this is the only pair of pants I have right now," he replied, giving me a significant look.

My cheeks flushed. "Oh. Right."

"And now that we've had that pleasant conversation," Will said, "maybe Hoot wants to tell us where we're going?"

"Not a chance," Hoot responded. "Like I told McKenzie, if we get caught, I don't want you knowin'."

"Fair enough." Will leaned back. His muscular arm was still draped around my shoulders.

"I suppose asking how long the drive is would basically be asking the same thing," I said, not sure if I should lean into him or not. I decided on 'sure' and rested my head on his shoulder again.

His smile said I made the right choice.

"You'd be correct. I ain't tellin' you nothin', just in case," Hoot replied.

"Sounds good," I conceded.

"I can tell you we're stoppin' at that gas station yonder. Suburban doesn't get as many miles to the gallon as a Camry. Might be a good time to visit the ladies' room," Hoot said.

"Okay." I adjusted my baseball cap on my head. So did Will.

Hoot frowned in the rearview mirror. "And we're gettin' you new hats. Ain't no Vikings this far south."

"Good point," Will agreed while I winced. We probably *should* have chosen something more generic.

Hoot pulled into the gas station and parked next to a pump. "Get me a Mountain Dew. Hell, get me three of 'em. We're gonna be drivin' for a while."

"Can do," Will responded, and we got out of the truck and headed into the store.

The attendant at this gas station looked a bit harried. She gave us the hairy eyeball when we started for the bathrooms. "You need a key."

"Oh." We walked back to the counter.

"And you need to buy something," she continued.

Will gestured outside. "We're buying gas."

She shrugged. "That's not gonna count today."

"What?!" I protested. "What do you mean? That's a *Suburban*. Do you have any idea how much we're going to be paying for gas?!"

"Don't care. Tired of you Yankee assholes messing up my bathrooms. I ain't cleaning that shit again," she said. "Not unless you buy something."

"You've got to be kidding me." I stared at her, wondering on what planet she wasn't going to get fired for this behavior.

As though she'd read my thoughts, she just shrugged. "Report me if you want to, but the boss is on vacation. Asshole makes enough off me to do that, you see, while I'm stuck here dealing with Yankees coming down all the time. For *their* vacations."

"We're not on vacation," Will said. "We're planning to stay." He turned on the charm full force, and I felt as though I should be wearing protective glasses. He leaned on the counter with a sexy smile. "Can't we just have the keys, please? I promise, we're here to stock up, too."

"Then stock up," the woman grunted, unmoved.

I would have given him my panties and my college tuition money if he'd turned that smile on me. That woman was a rock. "Okay, fine." I touched his shoulder, and we got two baskets and started filling them up.

Once we finished, we went to the register with our loaded baskets. The woman was still unimpressed. "I suppose you think you'll be getting into the bathrooms now."

"We were hoping so, yes," Will said.

The woman started ringing up our items. "I ain't cleaning up any mess again today. You can piss out on the side of the highway for all I care."

I gaped at her. "Lady, you've *got* to be joking. We're spending, like, three-hundred dollars here, with the gas and everything."

"Tough," she replied. "I don't see any of that."

Will began to reach into his pocket. I knew he was going for his money clip. I stopped him. It was the principle of the thing. "Look here, you…"

"What's takin' y'all so long?" Hoot asked, coming into the store. "I coulda taken a piss, shopped food, *and* learned to tap dance by now!"

"She won't let us use the bathroom," I said, pointing at the attendant. "First she said we had to stock up first. Then after we did, she said we still couldn't."

Hoot's eyes narrowed. "That so?"

"They're Yankees. They're gonna piss all over my walls," the woman complained.

"Maybe if you had a better disposition, they wouldn't," Hoot drawled. "Hand over the keys, or we're gonna make you check that stuff all back out and shelve it yourself."

The woman's jaw dropped. "You can't tell me what to do!"

"All right, kids. Let's go. We'll stop at the next place and get our goods." Hoot started for the door.

The woman reached under the counter and threw two sets of keys at us, one set that said 'Men's' and one that said 'Women's.' "Fine. You win. Just don't piss on my walls."

Hoot snapped up the Men's Room keys. "Come on, son. I ain't wrote my name on a wall in piss in a loooong time."

She squawked.

I bit back a grin. "Don't do it. She deserves a break, I think." I could be kind, now that I had the bathroom key in my hand.

"Hmph. Fine. But if I come back this way, I'm writin' 'Hoot' on that there counter in front of you," Hoot grumbled.

The woman gave me a grateful look.

Triumphant, we all went to the bathroom then went back to the Suburban with our spoils. Will and I now had generic hats with the American flag on them. They were Hoot approved.

However, when Will opened the back door for me, Hoot swore.

"Finding your inner feminist now?" Will teased him, but the look on Hoot's face silenced anything either of us would have said after that.

"Get in. Let's go. I don't like the look of that black sedan," Hoot said.

Will and I both followed Hoot's line of vision and saw a rather unassuming sedan sitting in a parking space on the side of the store. The disturbing thing about it was that its windows were so tinted, you couldn't see inside.

"Gonna have to switch vehicles sooner than I wanted to. Dang nabbit!" Hoot growled, hopping into the driver's seat.

I scrambled into the back of the Suburban and across the seat so Will wouldn't have to go around.

"Fuck, did he put a tracker up my ass or something?!" Will snapped as he jumped in and slammed the door closed.

"That'd sure be somethin'," Hoot said, throwing the truck into gear. "But I was told not to put anythin' past this guy."

Will looked at me. "Maybe we should separate. Hoot takes you to safety and…"

I shook my head vehemently. "No. You're coming with us. Hoot, tell him he's coming with us!"

"Don't make no difference now, I reckon. They've got our scent, whether we leave you by the side of the road or not. Ain't gonna stop 'em lookin' for McKenzie." Hoot took my side.

Will's shoulders slumped. "Fine."

"Reckon that busybody at the register called 'em. Bet your pictures are out to every gas station in every state in America by now," Hoot grumped. "Your pawpaw sure is a dick, Will *the Third*."

"Just Will," he sighed. "Fuck. *Fuck*."

Not knowing what else to do, I took his hand and squeezed it. "Look, like I said, you probably saved my life and my parents' lives by moving up your grandfather's timetable…"

"Life? Darlin', he's saved you from a fate worse'n death. Jake told me Will's pawpaw likes to play with his food," Hoot said. "And after bein' sent to prison, he must be angrier than a bear with his head in a hornet's nest."

"See? Fate worse than death," I echoed, squeezing Will's hand again. "So please, don't beat yourself up."

Will leaned his head back and squinched his eyes shut, clearly trying very hard to calm down. "I'm still going to feel guilty about Jake, Billy, and Horace for the rest of my life. You know that, right?"

I winced. "I don't blame you. I blame your grandfather."

"And that's squarely where you ought to leave the blame, too," Hoot piped up from the front seat.

Will grimaced but gave in with a slow exhale. "I'll leave it there. For now."

I threaded my fingers through his and leaned my head on his solid shoulder. "So, Hoot, where are we going to get another vehicle?"

"Dealership. I ain't got 'em parked all over the country, you know. We got a different one waitin' where we're goin', but we got to ditch this one *now*." Hoot shook his head and scowled in the rearview mirror. "And damned if that there sedan ain't followin' us now."

Will and I craned our heads around. "Where?"

"'Bout six cars back. Thinkin' they're bein' all stealth and what have you. Morons," Hoot snorted.

We watched until the highway curved then spotted the car. Will cursed under his breath. "Great."

"And that's why we're lookin' for a dealership," Hoot said. "But I have to lose 'em first. Ain't gonna do no good if they're standin' there watchin' us buy the car."

"I have cash," Will offered.

"An' you're gonna be usin' it, cuz I'm pretty sure that ol' bitch at the gas station gave 'em my name," Hoot grunted. "How much you got left?"

"About five thousand," Will said.

"So just some walkin' around money, then," Hoot snickered. "It'll get us where we need to go. Don't worry."

I looked up into the rearview mirror and met Hoot's eyes. "Hey, Hoot?"

"Yeah, McKenzie?" he said.

"Thank you." I meant it with deepest sincerity.

Hoot smiled slightly and nodded. "You're welcome."

8
WALKIN' AROUND MONEY

Will

Hoot was a masterful driver. He drove the Suburban as though he was going for first prize at a NASCAR race. It didn't hurt that any smaller car seeing a Suburban coming up their tailpipe quickly got out of the way. The black sedan did not have the same intimidation factor.

But when we crossed three lanes of traffic and nearly caused a twenty-car pile-up to take an exit, I decided he was crazy. The sedan wasn't able to follow us, of course, but I'd been pretty sure in those few seconds that we were all going to die.

"Y'all can stop hangin' off the oh-shit bars. Scary part's over," Hoot said as we joined traffic at a busy intersection. He frowned at the gas station on the corner. "Y'all keep your heads down. I ain't sure who all's been given a picture of you two in this area."

I ducked down and so did McKenzie. I curled my torso over hers.

Hoot got us to a Ford dealership, but that was all I knew because I saw the tall sign. He turned back and held out his hand. "Cash."

I fished my money clip out of my pocket and handed it over.

"Stay down until I tell you." He got out of the Suburban and locked us in.

The thunk of the locks engaging had a sound of finality to them. It made me feel both safe and vulnerable at the same time. If someone got those keys from him, we were sitting ducks.

"Want something to eat?" McKenzie asked, breaking the tense silence.

"Might as well, I suppose," I said after a beat. It would be a distraction, anyway.

She rummaged in the bag on the floor and came up with my Funyuns.

I smiled. "You hate those."

"I know. But you don't." She opened the bag and handed them to me. "Try not to get crumbs in my hair, okay?"

I laughed. "I'll do my best." I crunched into a Funyun, taking great care with the crumbs. It was harder than it sounded.

McKenzie got out some of her dark chocolate with chili, and I had to laugh again. "The only things we don't agree on."

"Well, that and your overwhelming sense of guilt, but who's counting?" she said.

I knew she was trying to tease me, but I still felt a heaviness in my soul.

"Will?" she prompted after I was quiet for a long time.

"Hmm?" I responded, trying to pretend like everything was okay. But we were hunched over in a Suburban so no one would recognize us, and there was at least one black sedan of baddies on our tail. Not to mention the fact that her uncles were dead.

She squeezed my knee. "Please stop brooding. Even Hoot says you saved me. I understand saving my life had a high cost, and I feel guilty about that, too, but we really do need to place the blame on your grandfather."

"Oh, trust me, there's plenty to go around," I said.

McKenzie sat up, which forced me to sit up as well.

"We can't—" I protested.

She brushed the Funyun crumbs off my lips. "I have a solution," she informed me.

I swallowed, hoping this was going where I thought it was going. "Really? What's that?"

McKenzie put her hands on my shoulders, leaned in, and kissed me.

It was a sweet, closed-mouth kiss. At first.

Then I licked her lips, tasting the dark, tangy sweetness there, and she opened up for me.

As soon as she allowed me entry, my tongue was in her mouth, desperately tangling with hers. My dick strained in my pants, swelling painfully against my fly. I wanted her. I wanted all of her. I wanted to consume and savor her just like the dark, spicy chocolate I could taste on her tongue.

She shifted into my lap, grinding right where I wanted her. I tore my mouth away and groaned. "We can't do it here," I panted, even while I slid a hand up her shirt to cup her breast through her lacy bra. "God… I want you."

"Me, too," she breathed. She kept grinding against my fly.

I gripped her ass, not sure if I wanted to stop her or help her along. I chose the latter. "When we get somewhere safe, I'm going to do things to you…" I promised, nibbling along her collarbone while helping her ride my bulge.

"Yeah?" She was close. I could tell in the way her body tensed.

That was good because I was close, too. And right then, I didn't give a damn about my pants. "That's it, honeybee. Just like that."

"'Honeybee'?" she repeated with a lilt of humor in her tone. But she didn't stop, thank God.

"Mhm. Your hair… beautiful… you're so beautiful," I babbled, not even capable of complete sentences anymore.

McKenzie bit down on her lip, and I thought she might be stifling a chuckle until I felt her body shudder against mine.

I exploded in my pants, groaning, my face pillowed against her shirt between her breasts. "Sonofabitch."

"That's not nearly as nice as 'honeybee,'" she grinned, clinging to my shoulders as we both came down.

I snorted. "As though I'd ever call you anything less than perfect."

She gave me a heart-melting expression, and I knew then and there I was never going to be satisfied. I was going to want this woman every moment of every second of every day for the rest of my damn life. When she ran her fingers through my hair, I wanted to purr.

"I think you're perfect, too," she murmured.

There was a knock on the window, and we both jumped. "Hoot —!"

It was not Hoot.

A man in an expensive suit smiled at us like the cat who got the cream. "Open up," he said.

"No," I replied, wrapping my arms around McKenzie and holding her protectively against my chest.

He frowned. "I'm not asking."

"I don't care," I said.

He opened his jacket, revealing a gun. "Don't make me use this—"

I reached behind me for my own gun, hoping I didn't shoot myself in the ass. Luckily, a gun appeared at the man's temple while I was fumbling for mine.

"What did I say about stayin' down?" Hoot admonished us.

The man raised his hands and started backing away.

"McKenzie, Will, get out of the truck. Go inside. I need to have a conversation with this here gentleman," Hoot said.

She leaned over and scooted out of the opposite door with me right behind her. I wondered what Hoot was going to do while we were gone, but most importantly, I wanted to get McKenzie to safety.

"Is Hoot going to be okay?" she asked once we were in the dealership.

"If anyone's going to be okay, it's going to be Hoot," I responded with confidence. I looked out the dealership windows, wondering where the black sedan could have parked.

Not seeing it, I looked over at her instead.

"I don't see it either," she said before I could ask.

"Weird." I was about to say something else when a salesman approached us.

"Good afternoon. Can I interest you in a..." He paused and looked us up and down.

We'd been recognized. "What's the reward?" I asked flatly.

"Fifty-million dollars for one, a hundred-million for both," the salesman said, licking his lips.

That wouldn't have been too rich for my blood a couple of weeks ago, but now that I was on the run, I only had five-thousand dollars to my name. "I suppose it wouldn't work to appeal to your better nature?" I tried.

The man pulled a cell phone from his pocket. "Not one bit."

Fantastic. Even if we managed to get away with Hoot, this dealership would know which car he had bought. "Look, I can't pay you now, but..."

"Too bad for you," the salesman said. "Hey, I found what you're looking f—"

There was a loud bang. I could have assumed it was a car backfiring, but that was unlikely. It was followed by several other loud bangs.

Hoot then rounded the corner of the dealership with blood splattered on his shirt and face. "How're you two?" he asked us.

"Our new friend here was just making a call on a hundred-million-dollar ransom," I said.

All three sets of eyes narrowed on the salesman.

"That so?" Hoot replied icily, tapping his gun against his thigh.

The salesman dropped his phone. It bounced and cracked on the ground. "Nothing. I wasn't doing anything. I swear!"

"You were giving us up to William Masterson Sr.," McKenzie accused him.

The man looked confused. "Who?"

"The guy paying the ransom. Don't play dumb," I growled.

"No... it's just... no. The guy... he didn't say his name was Masterson. He didn't even say he was working for Masterson," the man said.

Hoot stepped up to the salesman and put his gun under his chin. "Who, then?"

People had finally started to notice us. Dealer employees were eyeing us with greed while customers stared at us in fear. Phones were out everywhere, recording, calling. At least twenty people had seen us now.

"Uh... Hoot..." I began.

He ignored me and ground the muzzle of the gun harder into the underside of the salesman's chin. "Who?"

"I-Ibrahim. Ibrahim Abadi," the man squeaked.

Hoot frowned. "Who in tarnation is that?"

"He works for the sheik," I remembered from my grandfather's files.

"The sheik?" Hoot's lips pressed together in a thin line. "Them there gentlemen were working for Masterson. Were."

"Are-are they dead?" McKenzie asked.

"Reckon so. They shouldn't have been followin' us in the first place. That's what you get for threatenin' us," Hoot said. He looked at her. "You're gonna need to get more comfortable with shootin' and killin'. It's only gonna get worse from here."

She paled briefly then squared her shoulders and nodded.

"What do we do from here?" I asked.

Hoot took his gun away from the salesman's chin. "We leave." He looked around at our audience. "Fast as we can." He held out his hand to the salesman. "Keys."

"To what?" he asked.

"*Any* keys," Hoot demanded.

The salesman dug in his pocket and three sets of keys fell out.

"That'll do." Hoot snatched up a fob and herded us out of the dealership. He fired a shot at the ceiling. "Anyone follows us, they gonna meet their maker today."

No one followed us.

Hoot held the fob up in the air and pressed the lock button.

A brilliant blue Mustang flickered its lights at us.

"Get in the car," he said.

He didn't need to tell us twice. I rocked the passenger seat forward so McKenzie and I could get in the back of the two-door Mustang. I didn't have a lot of leg room once the passenger seat rocked back, but I wasn't about to complain to Hoot. Not while he was in this mood.

"We're sorry we didn't keep our heads down," McKenzie apologized as we tore out of the dealership.

"Nah. It's my fault. Shoulda found a different way to change cars. We're gonna have to do it again soon. You bet your ass this car's being reported to your Ibra-whoever or the police or both. We've gotta make a real run for it now," Hoot sighed. "They woulda caught you in the Suburban whether you were down or not. They recognized the truck. You were sucking face anyway. It's not like they would be able to see what you look like."

I felt heat creep up my neck. "We were—"

He waved a hand. "We got bigger problems now. I want you to tell me everything you know about this sheik and Ibra-whose-it."

9
IBRA-WHOSE-IT

McKenzie

I listened to Will give Hoot what little information he had. And it was definitely very little.

"I just know he and my grandfather conspired together to create a bounty on Caleb and Jocelyn Killeen," Will explained. "This sheik guy… I didn't get a lot of time to look into him, but I think they had something on him, too. Whoever he is, he is definitely not a good person. And his right hand man who was corresponding with my grandfather over the ransom was Ibrahim Abadi."

"We know a few things, then. Probably all we need to know," Hoot said. "He's rich, he's powerful, and he wants you two."

"McKenzie for sure," Will agreed.

"Don't kid yourself. These power-grabbin' types, they don't mind havin' just that little bit more to dangle over the competition's head," Hoot replied. "And that's what I'm thinkin'. Figure they're probably both doin' that illegal shit that Jack said Caleb and Jacey got roped into."

I raised my hand. "Question."

Hoot looked in the rearview mirror. "Yeah?"

"How much did Jack tell you about my parents? Because, until a couple of days ago, I thought they were boring farm folk," I said.

"Jack didn't have time to tell me much, but he did say they testified against this Masterson guy and that's why Will showed up out of the blue. Least that's what he was assumin'," he responded.

"I found a bunch of files on Ike's—my *grandfather's* right hand man—assistant's computer. I just had to meet them. My grandfather was obsessed with making their lives miserable. And now that he's getting out in two months, I have every reason to believe he's going to try to do it again." Will balled his hands into angry fists. "There were... he did... unspeakable things."

"Yeah, like make Jacey have you," Hoot said.

I blinked. "Excuse me?"

"Your mama carried him," he continued before Will could get a word out.

Horror choked me. "Oh my God, are you my *brother?!*" We'd kissed! We'd gotten each other off, for the love of Christ!

"No. No!" Will shook his head vehemently. "My grandfather took a donor egg and my dad's sperm and made me. I'm basically a test tube baby. He made your mom carry me to term. But no, we're not related. Not at all." He paused, then hunched his shoulders. "Would have been nice if they'd had a leg to stand on in court, though. The trial transcripts said they wanted me anyway."

It was weird. It was super weird, and I didn't even know what to begin to feel about it. "So, you put your tongue down my throat and decided not to tell me this?"

"Sorry," he mumbled. "I wasn't thinking."

"I don't even know what to *do* with this information! What do they even call a situation like this? Are you like... my stepbrother or something?!" I burst out.

"Oh, that'd be par for the course," Hoot chuckled.

"Why are you laughing?!" I snapped.

Hoot shrugged. "Your parents were step-siblings. Your grandma, Caleb's mom, married your pawpaw, Jacey's father, when Jacey was fifteen. They got together when she was eighteen, which was also when this all started."

"Thirty years ago." I gave Will the side-eye, and he had the decency to flinch. "I really wasn't thinking about that," he apologized.

"It's kind of a big thing to forget." I crossed my arms over my chest. "I feel like there should be a banjo playing in the background of all this. My parents were step-siblings, and I almost jumped... still don't know what to call you."

"Will." Will shrugged helplessly. "You just call me Will. Don't overthink it too much. Please."

I stabbed a finger into his chest. "I'm not talking to you."

"But you just said—"

"Never mind what I said!" I interrupted Will. "I just... I need a minute to get my head around this."

"We're hittin' the rest stop up yonder." Hoot nodded his head in the direction of a blue sign. "You've got that long to work things out. We need to switch vehicles, and that's gonna be the best place to do it."

I harrumphed and looked out my window, pointedly not looking at Will.

When we stopped, I jumped out of the Mustang and stormed off to the bathrooms, pulling my baseball cap low over my forehead. To my consternation, Will followed me.

"The men's room is on the other side," I informed him, pointing.

"Please let me apologize. I don't... I never thought of you that way. That's why I didn't say anything—because it doesn't matter to me. It's not even a big enough issue to—" He stopped when he saw the expression on my face. "But, obviously, you have different thoughts on the matter..."

"I don't know what to think right now. I would have appreciated knowing, though. I mean, it's... weird," I said.

Will sighed. "We don't have the same parents, and your mother was forced to carry me eleven years before you were even born. I think that was a violation of everyone's rights. It's part of what drove my father to suicide—my grandfather's treatment of Jacey and Caleb. I was shocked about all the other things I was finding out about my grandfather, but it didn't shock me at all that two good people who loved each other decided to have a child of their own. I suppose, if they'd won custody of me, and we'd grown up together, yeah, it'd be weird. I don't think it's weird. I think it's just life."

I scowled at him. "'Just life'? Really?"

"I'll... let you think about it some more. I'll see you in a bit." He went around the building to the men's rooms.

I went into one of the women's stalls and slammed the door. *Ugh!*

The stall had a box of those toilet seat liners at the back, so I pulled one out, placed it carefully on the seat, and sat down, my mind twirling. *Not a big deal? Just life?!*

A part of me wondered if wanting Will was disgusting now. Except I wasn't disgusted. Like he'd said, we weren't related at all.

We were strangers.

I shook my head. No, we weren't that, either. We'd found out a lot more about each other in the last few days than some people did in a lifetime. For instance, I knew Will was protective, principled, educated, and had bad taste in chips. He was kind, thoughtful... attractive. But not because he was smoking hot, which he was. More because he was a good person.

Also, I knew Will hadn't been born out of love, like I had. I thought it was admirable that my parents had still wanted him, but my eighteen-year-old mother being forced to be a surrogate? What kind of sick bastard did that?

Apparently, Will's grandfather.

I wondered what kind of a burden that was, knowing the only person left in the world who was supposed to love you was actually a selfish asshole who just wanted a copy of himself to succeed him in his bad dealings. It was remarkable Will hadn't considered going the same way his father had.

Or maybe he had considered it?

It was that thought that had me rushing out of the bathroom and over to the men's room. I'd gone so fast that I'd splashed water on my shirt when I washed my hands. I got a lot of leering glances, and I could only imagine how see-through my shirt had become.

Will was at one of the sinks. He looked at me in the mirror, closed his eyes, opened them, then turned around. "I hope that's not how you look when you're about to turn me down cold."

"You're not going to kill yourself, are you?" I blurted.

"What?" He gaped at me. "No. I'm not going to kill myself. Whatever gave you that idea?"

"Because your dad and your grandfather and all this and everything." I gestured vaguely in the air. "You know."

Will smiled sadly. He took off his sweater, flashing the best set of abs I'd ever seen in person, and handed it over to me. "Here. You need this for now. I think these truckers want to eat you alive."

I didn't take the sweater. I was too busy looking at how well he filled out his T-shirt. It was straining to keep all his muscles from popping out. "You must spend a lot of time at the gym."

"I didn't have much else to keep me occupied, since Ike was doing everything that wasn't public-facing. I should have questioned that more." He shook the sweater at me. "Please put this on. I promise we can burn your bra or whatever you'd like to do in protest of the patriarchy when we aren't... here."

"I'm not going to walk around topless, if that's what you're worried ab—holy crap." I saw myself in the mirror behind Will and quickly yanked his sweater on.

He relaxed. "Okay, so, did you decide what to call me yet?"

"Still working on that. You didn't answer my question. What about all that's happened to you? You're really not considering ending it all, right?" I asked, rolling up the long sleeves of his sweater. It hung on me everywhere except my boobs and ass.

"After everything, sure. I thought about it. But what good did my father killing himself do anybody? He could have testified against my grandfather. Instead, he left that burden on your parents." Will gestured for me to walk ahead of him. "And now we're in this mess. I'm sure my father could have done a much better job of dismantling my grandfather's enterprises, but he didn't. And your parents couldn't. And maybe I can't, either, but I'll be damned if I don't at least try."

"I think your father must have not seen any other way out. Don't blame him," I said quietly.

"I don't. I blame my grandfather for making him feel so trapped." We walked back to the parking lot.

There was no sign of Hoot. Or the Mustang.

"What in the…?" I gasped.

"This can't be good," Will said.

As though expecting it might magically appear, we walked over to where the Mustang had been. There was a set of skid marks, but otherwise nothing. No note. No clue.

"I'll bet they found him," I whispered. "I'll bet he took off to make them think we were still in the car with him."

"That would make sense. But we have a big problem now," he replied.

"Hoot's gone, and we have no idea where to go from here?" I said.

"Yes. That and Hoot has my money." He locked eyes with me.

My jaw dropped. "Oh my God. We're stranded."

"I've still got my bank card, but I wouldn't be surprised if my grandfather found a way to shut it down," he sighed, rubbing the back of his neck. "And if I use it, it'll flag our location."

I glanced at the rest stop building. "Is there an ATM in there?"

"Did you miss the part where I said it'll flag our location?" Will raised an eyebrow.

"Just take out as much money as it'll let you. I'll see if someone will let us use their phone to call a cab," I said.

"A cab to where?" he asked.

"Anywhere but here," I answered.

10
ANYWHERE BUT HERE

Will

I went to the ATM filled with dread. I was certain my grandfather had found the account. Absolutely positive. The question was, had he disabled it, or was he just tracking it?

It wasn't as though we had any choice in the matter. I was going to have to find out.

I took my card out of my wallet and placed it in the slot, wondering if the ATM was about to eat and shred it.

To my surprise, it didn't. In fact, it even recognized my PIN.

When the screen came up showing my balance, every penny was there. I just stared at the six-million dollars for a moment.

"It's not going to let you withdraw all that. Just pull up to your limit and let's go," McKenzie said anxiously.

"Right." I checked my options then pulled out fifteen-hundred dollars. "That's the limit."

"That'll get us somewhere else." She grabbed my arm as I was shoving the roll of bills into my pocket.

Outside the rest stop building, she took my sweater off.

"Um… McKenzie. Your shirt hasn't dried yet," I informed her politely.

"That's the idea." She let go of my arm and sidled over to a trucker standing next to his rig. "Hi," she purred in a tone that made my dick perk up and pay attention. "I was wondering if I could use your phone to call a cab."

The trucker made eye contact with her chest. "You don't need no cab, little missy. There's plenty of room in my rig."

"Aww, that's nice of you. But my boyfriend and I are traveling together, and I'm not sure you want us *both* riding with you," she said, her voice still sultry.

He looked at me, then at McKenzie's boobs, then back at me again. "Well, I don't know…"

"Pretty *please* let me use your phone?" she asked, thrusting out her chest a little bit.

The trucker got a look on his face I didn't like. "Show me your tits and it's yours."

She froze.

"Aaaand that's the end of that experi—" I began.

McKenzie stripped her shirt off, leaving her in the white lacy bra I'd felt up only hours ago. "Happy?"

"Honey, I said your tits, not your bra," the trucker drawled.

I was too shocked to move until she reached around to the clasp at her back. "McKenzie, it's not worth i—"

The clasp popped open, and she slid the bra off, dangling it from her fingertips as she let the trucker—and me—look all we wanted to.

All my dick wanted now was to get out of my pants. My brain went completely blank except maybe for the word 'boobs' on repeat as I stared at the most perfect pair of pink-tipped DDs I'd ever seen in my life.

"Happy now?" she asked angrily.

"Fuck me. I'll be jerking myself off to those for months," he breathed and the same thought crossed my mind.

Only I was never going to be satisfied just jerking off and imagining them. I was going to get my cock between them and titty fuck her. If she'd let me, of course.

She was still trying to figure out if we were 'gross.'

It was that thought that brought me back to my senses. I strode over and wrapped my sweater protectively over her front. "Okay. You've seen enough. Phone?" I seethed.

"I don't know what you got going on with this one, but I can do it better," he grinned at McKenzie, who flinched. But, true to his word, he produced his phone from his back pocket. "Keep it. That show was worth a billion of them. Code's 957326."

"Thank you!" she chirped, recovering her flirtatiousness. Then I steered her away from the rig, trying not to imagine what the trucker was about to do when he got into his cab.

"Ugh," she said when we were out of hearing range, pulling her shirt and my sweater on. "I don't get it. They're just boob—are you seriously hard right now?!"

I grimaced. "Yes. If you didn't want me to be, you shouldn't have shown me the most fantastic breasts I've ever seen."

McKenzie blushed, from embarrassment or anger, or perhaps both. "Thank you for the compliment, but I still don't know where I am with you."

"You know where you are with me," I said huskily.

She shivered, and I could tell it was attraction and not revulsion that made her do so. "Will…"

"Yes?" I murmured.

McKenzie swallowed. "We… we need to call that cab and split."

"I'll take that as a 'we'll table this conversation for later,'" I chuckled.

She blushed again and stabbed the code into the phone. Then she started googling cab companies near us.

It took a few phone calls to find one that would take cash and not a card up front, but after a nail-biting half hour, a beat-up old cab showed up at the rest stop.

"Lose your ride?" the driver asked as we got in.

I handed her five-hundred dollars. "However far this gets us in any direction but North, that's where we want to go."

Her eyes widened, and she pocketed the cash. "Here I thought you might stiff me when you wouldn't give your credit card over the phone, but I see you're a man of your word. Guess we're goin' West to Austin. I've got family that way I can visit after I drop you off."

"Sounds great." I sat back in the taxi. To my surprise, McKenzie leaned against me.

"Do you mind if I take a nap?" she asked tiredly.

Come to think of it, neither of us had gotten much sleep over the last few days. But I wasn't willing to let us both be asleep when there was potential danger all around us. "You can sleep. I'm going to stay up for a while."

"Okay. Thank you." She snuggled into me and quickly dropped off into a deep sleep.

The cab driver raised an eyebrow at me in the rearview mirror. "Ain't she a bit young for you?"

"She is. But she doesn't seem to mind," I replied.

"I gotta say. You two are cuter than a puddle of puppies," she said.

Something niggled at the back of my mind. That was an odd phrase. "Thank you."

"Don't thank me yet. We ain't in Austin, yet." She turned to concentrate on the road.

Puddle of puppies. Puddle of puppies. It was such a weird saying. But I'd heard it before, which made it even more odd. Where had I heard it before?

McKenzie shifted and cuddled closer to me, her hand moving to rest high on my thigh. I was pretty sure she hadn't done it on purpose, but my cock didn't care. The 'puddle of puppies' conundrum completely fled my mind.

I worked on evening out my breathing and thinking of gentle streams and falling leaves to try to calm my body down. I was only marginally successful.

Our cab driver whistled to herself as the hours crawled by. The taxi was moving fast, but time was moving slow. All I wanted was to be in a hotel, motel, or hostel or wherever we were going to end up and beg McKenzie to have me. This surrogate thing wasn't really *that* big of a deal. Was it?

"We're just about there," the cab driver interrupted my thoughts.

I glanced out at the landscape. It was still a bunch of scrub grass and widely-scattered buildings. "This doesn't look like the city."

"Will, we ain't goin' to the city," the cab driver said.

I frowned. "How did you know my name?"

"You're really pretty naive. Both of you." The cab driver's accent was gone.

Puddle of puppies. It was a phrase my *grandfather* used! I hadn't ever heard anyone else use that phrase. "You're working for my grandfather."

"What?!" McKenzie gasped, coming awake. Her hand briefly brushed my fly as she drew it back, but that wasn't at the forefront of my mind anymore.

"Bingo. Give the man a prize. And I've got both of you. It was so fucking easy it ought to be criminal," the cab driver laughed. "Easiest hundred-mil I'll ever make."

Fuck.

"Shit!" McKenzie reached for a door handle, but the cab driver locked it. I noticed the manual locks were missing from the back seat.

"Hey now," the cab driver said. "We're going about eighty. You don't want to be a splat on the road, do you?"

McKenzie stopped jiggling the handle.

I reached for my gun.

The cab driver pulled out her own and pointed it into the back seat, right at McKenzie. I didn't know how she could do that and keep driving. She must have been some sort of professional. "Guns, please. Throw them up front."

With a growl of frustration, I tossed my gun onto the floor of the passenger seat.

"McKenzie?" the cab driver prompted like a school teacher asking for math homework.

McKenzie sighed and tossed her own gun up front. It landed next to mine.

"Great. Now we can be friends." She put her gun away. "I suppose you wouldn't know that your grandfather has a facility out here, would you, Will?"

A facility in the middle of nowhere? Somehow, it didn't surprise me. "I didn't know, no."

"It's the perfect place to keep you until someone comes to get you," the cab driver went on. "I think your grandfather develops chemical weapons or some other such thing there. But as long as you stay in your rooms, I don't think there's any danger."

Chemical weapons. *Great, another terrible, illegal thing he's doing.* "Great."

"Are we just going to go along with this?!" McKenzie gaped.

"We don't have a lot of choices right now," I replied quietly.

"There's the brains of the operation." The cab driver smiled at us in the rearview mirror. "Unless you want to be the dead part of 'dead-or-alive,' McKenzie, I'd suggest you follow Will's lead."

McKenzie sagged next to me.

"It's just for now," I whispered. "We'll escape later."

"How?" she lamented.

The phone the trucker had given us rang.

"Answer it. It's probably your grandfather," the cab driver chuckled.

I glowered at her, but answered the phone. "Hello?"

"Don't say my name. You wearin' your seat belts?" Hoot asked.

I blinked and looked at McKenzie. "Yes."

"Good. Hand the phone to the nice lady driver," he said.

Raising my eyebrows, I held out the phone to the cab driver. "It's for you."

"Good. I can give them my account and routing numbers." The cab driver laughed. She turned in her seat to grab the phone.

Something slammed hard into the rear of the cab. The phone flew from my hand as the cab went spinning.

"Fucking *what?!*" the cab driver yelled, turning back and wrestling with the wheel.

"Fucking Hoot," I managed to get out before the seat belt locked across my chest, restraining my words.

The cab driver had just managed to get the taxi back under control when there was another bang against the back bumper. She fiddled desperately with her seat belt but was unable to engage it before the third ram to the back of the cab sent us in a dizzying whirl.

McKenzie grabbed my hand as the cab rolled, then flipped end over end when it hit the ditch. The driver was thrown from the car, launched straight out of the windshield, her blood the only reminder she'd been there at all.

I squeezed McKenzie's hand for all I was worth, begging God to at least let her be okay. The cab finally rocked to a stop, and she and I dangled upside-down from our seatbelts.

"Jesus," I rasped. I could see scratches from glass on her face when I looked over. "McKenzie, are you okay?"

She was breathing hard. Her eyes, which had been squeezed shut, looked at me. "Your face…" she said. "Your arms…"

"Fuck that. Are *you* okay?" I asked again.

"I… think so?" She rolled her neck.

Our hands still clutched each other. I had no intention of letting go.

"I'm fine, too, as far as I can tell." I glanced out the shattered window and jumped. "Hoot!"

"Nothing broken?" he asked.

"No, no thanks to you," I grumbled.

Hoot shrugged. "I figured you'd rather get killed than whatever your pawpaw has in store for you. Luckily, you didn't." He took out a pocket knife and slashed my seatbelt.

I fell onto the cab ceiling. "Ow."

"Suck it up, buttercup. Can you catch McKenzie?" he asked.

I nodded and got into position.

Hoot went around and cut her seatbelt as well. She landed on me, which was better than her landing on the twisted metal of the roof.

"Let's go," he said.

11

BACK WITH HOOT

McKenzie

I didn't want to look at the mangled mess that was the cab driver. It seemed wrong somehow that we hadn't even gotten her name. Now? She was unrecognizable.

Hoot, on the other hand, walked right over to her, ignored a bone protruding through her thigh, and fished around in her left pocket.

"What are you doing?!" I gasped.

"You paid her good money, didn't you?" he replied. "I'm gettin' it back."

"She can keep the money. Really. Funeral expenses or something." Will wheezed, looking at the same morbid scene I was.

"Funeral expenses my ass. She ain't takin' any more time, trouble, *or* money from any of us. Got me a scratch on my grill now." Hoot grunted. He tried the right pocket and seized a handful of bloody money. "Ha! There it is."

Will made an urping sound but didn't throw up. I felt the same way, though I wasn't sure I'd be able to hold back.

"I think I'm going to be sick," I whispered.

"Well, hurry up'n be sick," Hoot said. "We got places to be."

I turned to the side and threw up. Will quickly grabbed my hair. He rubbed my back with his other hand.

Hoot offered me a handkerchief. "There, now that's over, get in the truck."

The 'truck' was a brand new black Escalade with a front grate. No wonder he'd been able to ram the cab so easily without being damaged.

I wiped my mouth, and we headed over to the Escalade. Will and I slid into the back. I noticed there was another row of seating, but I decided to stay by Will. Maybe I hadn't made up my mind yet, but he felt safe. And sane. I was starting to wonder about Hoot, especially when he shoved the bloody five-hundred dollars into his pocket.

Bile rose in the back of my throat.

"Don't you go messin' up my truck. We ain't stoppin' to air 'er out." The man in question admonished me. He handed back a cold bottle of Sprite. "Thought we might be needin' this at some point."

I took the Sprite and sipped it, trying to get my stomach to calm down.

Will rubbed my back again. "It's over now," he murmured. "Just breathe."

Tears welled in my eyes, and I dashed them away. "It's not over. We're still being chased by everybody on the planet."

"True," Will conceded.

"Eh, not everyone. Y'all got me," Hoot grinned.

His words were comforting and frightening at the same time. "Thanks, Hoot," I said just the same.

Hoot nodded and started away from the scene of the accident just as sirens began wailing in the distance. "Gotta get us outta here before them cops see you. Bet you anythin' they've got pictures of you, too."

"Great," Will sighed.

"Your pawpaw is a piece of work," Hoot said. "But now we got this Ibra-whose-it on us, too."

"And the Trinary," Will mumbled.

I looked at him. "The what?"

"My grandfather hires the Trinary a lot to do his dirty work. Or, rather, he did. It's been thirty years. They've probably retired," Will continued.

"You don't sound so sure, son," Hoot said.

"I'm not. I'm not really sure about anything, except that my grandfather is a monster, and he wants to eat us for lunch," Will responded.

I put a hand on his knee. "We're going to find my parents, eventually. And we'll get to some proper authorities who care about taking your grandfather down. You'll testify, and things will be okay again."

"That's all a long way off," Hoot informed us. "Right now, my priority is keepin' y'all safe. I don't know where your parents went. Jake didn't, either. We got to worry about your grandparents and your uncle, too."

"Who?" I asked, confused.

"The rest of your family. Y'all don't think Masterson's just gonna leave 'em alone, do you?" Hoot said.

Will's face hardened, and I wondered what I was missing. "Maybe we don't care what happens to them. All right, maybe the uncle, but..."

"You're telling me my grandpa and grandma are still alive? The ones who got married and made it so my parents met each other?" I interrupted.

"They're in witness protection, but yeah. Jake didn't know where. Their name was Collins. That was your mama's last name." Hoot nodded along with what he was saying. "Your pa's last name is Killeen. But y'all go by Kent now, I know. Figure your pawpaw and family changed their last name, too."

I turned to Will. "Why wouldn't we want to help them?"

"Your grandfather hit your mother. He didn't think your parents should be together, and he tried to take Masterson's side and get their testimony thrown out in court. Jeanie, your grandmother, went along with it for a long time but broke in front of the judge. It's all written down," Will said. "They're not good people. I think your parents tried to get custody of their half-brother as well, but it didn't happen."

"He *hit* mom?!" I yelped.

"Yes, and tried to trap her in the house so she couldn't see Caleb.

He's an asshole, McKenzie. You don't need to feel beholden to them at all," Will gritted out.

I sat back in my seat, my mind reeling. "Maybe they've changed?" I said faintly.

"Doubt it," Hoot replied. "But they're family. Y'all don't just abandon family." He glared at Will in the rearview mirror. "*Some people don't know that.*"

"Hey. He doesn't *have* any real family," I defended him, taking his hand. "He's defended me a few times, and we're not even related."

Will let out a breath it seemed like he'd been holding a long time. "So, you've decided, then?"

"Decided what?" I asked.

"What I am to you?" he responded softly, squeezing my hand.

I blinked. I supposed I had. "I guess you're my boyfriend," I grumbled.

Will smiled. "What? I couldn't hear you."

"You're my boyfriend!" I all but yelled. "Happy now?"

"You have no idea," he replied in a gravely tone.

I got the impression Will would have liked to put his tongue back down my throat right then and there, so I swatted his chest. "Back off, big boy. I don't want to scandalize Hoot."

"Oh. Right. Hoot." Will looked up as though just remembering the man was there.

"We're stoppin' at a motel soon enough. Y'all can work out whatever this is when we get there," Hoot said, rolling his eyes.

I knew what we'd be doing when we got to the motel. From the look in Will's eyes, I knew neither of us were questioning it. Not anymore.

As the sky grew dark, anticipation bubbled in my stomach. My sexual experiences with my high school sweetheart had been very disappointing. But when I saw the way Will looked at me, and felt the sensual way he was rubbing his thumb on the back of my hand, I had no doubt he was about to rock my world.

Hoot pulled into a motel around ten o'clock. The sign was burned out except for the O in Motel. I giggled, thinking it was rather appropriate. I was about to have my very first male-induced one soon.

"Walls are paper thin in this place, I'm sure," Hoot observed. "Don't go makin' too much noise."

"Noted," Will said.

Then Hoot got out of the car. "Gettin' two rooms. Y'all wait here. I'll come back with the keys."

"Actual… keys?" Will asked, confused.

"Some places still use 'em," Hoot replied with a chuckle. "You probably ain't even been in a car that needs a key. You use them fob things all the time."

"I like old sports cars. I have a few," Will said defensively.

Hoot snorted. "Of course you do." He walked off to the main office.

"We're doing this, right?" Will asked once Hoot was gone.

"I'll be very disappointed if we don't," I responded softly.

Will gave me a sexy smile, which I saw in the dome light just before it switched off. It warmed me to my core. "I'll be very disappointed, too."

We sat there holding hands until Hoot came back. He handed us an honest-to-God key with a room number dangling off it. "I'm in the room next door. Y'all try to keep it down, all right?"

"Absolutely," Will promised.

I wasn't sure I could keep the same promise, but Will seemed sure, so I just nodded.

Hoot nodded back. We got out of the Escalade and headed to our respective rooms.

Once the door of Room 11 closed behind us, I was suddenly very nervous. I glanced at Will after he finished locking the door and engaging the chain.

"Hey," he said, walking over and wrapping me in his arms. "Nothing's going to happen tonight that you don't want. If you don't want to do anything, that's fine. If you want me to sleep in the bathtub, that's fine, too. I'd bunk with Hoot, but I don't want to leave you alone."

I leaned my head on his chest, listening to his heartbeat. It was steady and comforting. I knew he would touch me with respect and stop if I told him to. Just like I knew he was a good man and had poor taste in chips. "I don't want you to sleep in the tub."

"That's good to hear," he chuckled. He brushed a stray lock of hair off my face. "And?"

"And I want to have sex with you," I said boldly.

He drew a sharp breath and his heart began pounding in my ear. I could feel him harden through his pants. "That's even better," he replied, his tone gravely. "I... shit. I don't have a condom. Just... hold that thought. This seems like the type of place that would sell them at the front desk..."

"You don't need a condom," I told him.

Will raised an eyebrow. "You're nineteen. I assure you, I *do* need a condom."

"I have an IUD. Rough periods. Mom recommended it when I turned sixteen. It lasts five years," I explained.

He stared at me. "I am a very, *very* lucky sonofabitch."

"And you should know, I've only been with one guy. A few times. And it wasn't exactly... pleasant," I admitted.

"That shouldn't be a problem between us. I'm... pretty experienced. I won't give you my number, but it's up there," he shrugged. "Not bragging. Just a fact." He seemed about to say something more then changed his mind. "So, start with kissing?"

"Yeah." I closed my eyes and tilted my chin up.

Will cupped my cheek and fused his lips to mine. It was just like before, heat burning between us. We couldn't get close enough.

He grabbed my ass and ground my pelvis against his erection. I could feel through his pants it was big. My vagina quivered with anticipation.

"Will," I moaned against his lips. "I want you."

"I know, honeybee. I want you, too," he replied, nibbling my lower lip. He pulled his sweater off me, then my shirt.

My fingers trembling, I unbuttoned my jeans and toed off my

shoes and socks. When he saw me in just my underwear and bra, he licked his lips. "Take it *all* off." His voice was sultry.

It was an order I was happy to obey. If a little nervous. I unsnapped my bra and let the straps slide off my arms, falling to the floor.

His breathing hitched. "Fuck me… still the best breasts I've ever seen…" He squeezed his eyes shut. "I'm going to need you to get on the bed."

"I thought you wanted me to take my panties off?" I teased.

"I'll take care of it. Get on the bed," he said. "On your back."

I got on the bed and lay down on my back. To my surprise, he grabbed me by the ankles and tugged me right back down to the edge. "Will?" I asked, perplexed.

He stripped my panties off me then kissed his way up my leg, from my ankle to the inside of my thigh. "Honeybee," he replied huskily. "I need some honey."

"What do you—?!" Realization dawned when he knelt down and wedged his broad shoulders between my legs, spreading me wide open for him. "Oh my God, you're really going to…"

"I'm really going to," he confirmed. Then he pressed down on my hips to hold me in place and licked right up my wet seam.

12
SUBLIME

Will
    I knew she'd taste like honey.

13
BIG BOY

McKenzie

My high school sweetheart had always refused to go down on me, so I was shocked when Will's tongue penetrated my folds. It swirled around my clit, and he sucked on me there for a bit before teasing his tongue up inside me.

"W-Will..." I gasped, trying to arch but then realizing why he was holding my hips down. He had no intention of being dislodged or rushed.

I moaned as he tongue-fucked me, licking like I was the best candy he'd ever tasted. He even made yummy-yummy sounds, so I knew he was enjoying himself.

It completely blew my mind.

My hips bucked slightly despite being trapped by his strong hands, and I buried my hand in his dark hair, my whole body quivering. He was going to take me there. He was going to make me...

I came hard with a cry, completely forgetting about the thin walls. Will lapped up everything I gave him, seeing my body through every last tremble.

"Mmm, honeybee, you taste so good," he murmured, kissing the inside of my thigh after wringing every ounce of pleasure I had out of me.

Or so I thought.

He stood and looked down at me. I figured I must look like a hot mess, but he just smiled with lust burning in his eyes. "Beautiful," he whispered. Then he stripped his shirt over his head and tossed it aside.

I saw miles and miles of muscle that I suddenly wanted to touch. I reached for him.

Will took off his pants along with his boxers, and the most monstrous dick I'd ever seen sprang free.

My jaw dropped. "Holy cow." It wasn't as though I'd seen a lot of pornos or something, but I'd seen enough to know he'd have gotten top dollar.

He grinned at me as his stiff cock bobbed in front of him. "That's all because of you, honeybee."

"Jesus, good thing we're not doing a condom. How would we have ever found a size that fits?!" I gaped.

Will laughed. "Doing you without a condom? Highlight of my existence. Though, speaking of which, I think you might still be too tight for me."

"Ya think?" I snorted. "I wasn't expecting to be taking on the Empire State Building today."

"If you don't want to give me an even bigger head, I'd suggest you call him Lucille or something," he chuckled.

"I knew you were a big boy, but I didn't expect you'd be packing, you know, a Big Boy." Internally, I despaired. How was I even going to do this?

He leaned down over me, and I snapped my thighs shut out of self-preservation. "Shh," he said, rubbing his hand over my stomach and massaging my mound. "Just fingers. I don't want to hurt you any more than you want to be hurt. We can make this work, don't worry."

I shot him a warning glance then cautiously parted my legs.

True to his word, he pressed the heel of his hand over my clit, rubbing there, then pushed two fingers inside me when I widened my thighs even more.

I clung to his shoulders, a thrill of excitement going through my body as he brought me back to that place I hadn't expected I'd be visiting twice today. Who knew?

Apparently he did, because he wasn't at all surprised when my inner muscles clamped down on his fingers. This time, he fused his mouth to mine to swallow my cries of pleasure as I came apart.

That had to be it. I knew I wasn't capable of another one as I lie panting beneath him.

Of course, that was when he introduced a third thick finger, widening me even more. He hooked his fingers just right and a zing went through my whole body.

"Will... I don't know if I can..." I moaned while my nethers were still trying to decide if they liked finger three or not.

"I know you can. You've got the most responsive body I've ever seen. And it's all mine..." he purred, still finger-fucking me. His dick was a hard reminder against my thigh of what the ultimate goal was.

I was starting to feel like an Olympian training for the big day. I certainly wouldn't be falling off the horse. Still, I wasn't sure how much more my body could take. "Can we try now?" I asked.

"Now?" He frowned slightly. "Just... um... let me try something first, and we'll see."

Then his pinky entered me as well.

I arched my back. *Holy fuck!* My body protested loudly, even with him still thumbing my clit.

"Not sure that's the greatest idea. Like I said, I don't want to hurt you." He withdrew his fingers, and I wasn't sure if I was more relieved or disappointed.

"But—" I all but whined.

"Let's just play today. We'll have plenty more opportunities," he suggested.

I pouted. "I can do it."

"I've no doubt in my mind that you can. But I want you to enjoy it. Enjoy me. Hence, practice." He winked at me. "Okay, Rocky?"

"Hmph." I narrowed my eyes on him. "Fine, but I get to suck your dick."

"Deal," he replied eagerly.

"And I get to touch *allll* of that," I continued, gesturing to the wide expanse of his muscles.

"I really wish you would," he grinned.

"All right then. Now that's decided." I struggled to sit up, my body completely wrung out. He helped me.

"This is your fault, you know. You can't give a girl mind-blowing orgasms and expect her to still be in one piece when it's over," I complained.

Will's smile turned heart-meltingly sexy. "Who said it's over?" He sat down on the bed then laid on his back with his dick still at stiff attention. He beckoned me with one crooked finger. "All right, honeybee. Have your way with me."

It was as though he'd invited me to the world's best amusement park. I ran my hands over the bumps and crevices of his muscular body. His brown nipples begged to be tasted. So I did.

He groaned and spiked his fingers through my hair. Then he gently tugged me away by my hair. "Get on my lap. I want to play with your tits."

"But it's my turn," I pouted.

"And you'll get another one later, but if I don't get my mouth on those gorgeous nipples, I'm going to die," he assured me.

I rolled my eyes and straddled his waist. I imagined his dick was a bit disappointed I hadn't chosen that moment to take him all in.

"Lean forward. Feed them to me," he said, his voice husky.

I leaned down, and he palmed my breasts, pushing them together so he had better access to both nipples.

Then he did positively sinful things with his tongue and teeth. Sinful. I had never known one could get that kind of pleasure just from having their breasts played with.

My core clenched. Much to my bewilderment, I came again.

"Nice," he murmured, delivering one last lick. "I knew you'd be responsive."

"I didn't," I whimpered.

"Someone didn't do right by you. His loss." He rolled so I was on my back, pinned beneath him.

"Hey!" I objected. "My turn!"

Will fondled me intimately and I forgot it was anyone's turn at all. "I tell you what. I'll let you blow me next time."

"What?" I mumbled, nearly cross-eyed.

"You know what I want more?" he asked.

"More than a blowjob?" My mind tried to parse this idea. I couldn't remember my ex ever wanting anything more than he wanted a blowjob.

He nodded. "More than a blowjob."

"You want to put the tip in and cum?" I offered.

Will shivered. "That sounds fantastic, but not today. Today, I want to cum on your tits."

"You really do like my tits, don't you?" I wheezed as he kept pleasuring me with his fingers.

"I really, really do," he confirmed. "I'm going to titty fuck you, then finish on your boobs."

"Sounds messy," I teased, pretending to think about it.

He leaned down and whispered in my ear. "I'll clean you up after."

It was my turn to shiver. Then shuddered as my body clamped down on his fingers and I came again with a yowl.

"Hoot is going to be so disappointed with all the noise," Will laughed. He nibbled my neck. "But I'm not."

"I'd hate to disappoint you." This time, I wasn't teasing.

"Honeybee, even if we stopped right here, I got to taste you. I could die a happy man," he said.

I smiled at him. "Charmer."

"You know it." He straddled me, putting most of his weight on his knees, then pressed my breasts together.

I figured I could help. Before he could push his cock between my tits, I reached out and stroked it from base to tip. I couldn't get my hand all the way around it! But what I lacked in distance I made up for with enthusiasm.

Will groaned and shook, precum dripping from his tip onto my skin. "Honeybee, if you keep doing that, I'm going to cum on your face."

"So? Cum on my face," I responded boldly.

He let out a strained laugh then let go of my breasts so he could grab my wrist. "I tell you what. We'll explore every damn place I can come on or in you. But we've got time. And right now, I want to fuck your titties."

"So bossy," I grinned, but let go of his dick. I pressed my breasts together myself instead. "Like this?"

"Your last lover was a moron if he never tried this," he snorted, repositioning my hands just slightly. He took some of his leaking precum and got his cock wet. Then he threaded his fingers through mine, and we held my breasts together.

Will pressed his wet cock between my breasts. He began leaking more, which aided the smooth journey back and forth.

I felt powerful as his tip kept poking out in between a few inches. I locked eyes with him, then slowly licked the precum right off the tip of him on a down stroke.

"Jesus," he groaned. "Honeybee, I need you to close your eyes, just in case."

I closed my eyes, and sure enough, with a rough grunt, I felt Will's hot cum jet onto my chest and face.

"Open your mouth," he murmured.

Doing as he asked, I felt his hard tip bump against my lower lip. Then cum spurted into my mouth, and I coughed.

"Swallow it," he ordered.

That made me quiver all the way down to my core, and I did my best to swallow every drop of his stream.

Then it was over. We both panted in the aftermath, and I could feel the muscles of Will's legs twitch on either side of me.

"Shower," he said, his voice no longer harsh and authoritative.

"Can I open my eyes yet?" I asked, reaching up to wipe cum away.

He stopped my hands. "No. Keep them closed."

"How am I supposed to see where I'm g—" The rest ended in a

shriek of surprise as the bed rocked and then he hoisted me over his shoulder. "Will!"

Will spanked my ass lightly. "Hush. Let me take care of you."

I moaned. *Okay, so apparently I like spanking.* Or maybe it was just that I was so overstimulated.

"Good girl." He carried me into what I assumed was a very seedy bathroom, but I also trusted him not to let me step in or on anything gross. Hell, I trusted him completely.

He started the water without even having to put me down. I could hear it run. And run. And run.

Will swore. "Okay, honeybee, I'm afraid we're in for a lukewarm experience."

I made a face. "Great."

"We'll just have to make up for it with body heat," he decided.

I froze. "We're going to do more?!"

He chuckled. "You bet your sweet pink bottom we're doing more."

14

SWEET PINK BOTTOM

Will

The next day, Hoot smirked at us as we walked out of our hotel room. Well, I walked. McKenzie sort of sauntered like a saddle-sore cowboy. She kept casting dirty looks my way, especially when she had to sit down gingerly in the Escalade.

And I hadn't even been inside her yet.

Then again, I did have pretty big fingers and a wicked tongue. No doubt she would sleep in the SUV, on my shoulder again.

God help me, I could still taste her sweet honey on my lips.

"Problems, honeybee?" I asked innocently as I sat down next to her.

"You know what you did," she hissed.

I grinned. "I remember everything *we* did."

"You don't have to be so satisfied with yourself," she grumbled, folding her arms over her chest. She winced and unfolded them. Yes, like the perfect little nip on her neck, her nipples were now swollen and sensitive from my attention. I almost felt bad for her, but I'd had my own challenges putting a shirt on today.

"Seems you two worked things out," Hoot said from the front seat, finally letting out a rolling chuckle.

"We worked things out a few times. You have to make sure to get it right, after all," I replied, sending a teasing look her way.

"You got it right the first time," she huffed. "The rest was just…"

"Mind-blowing?" I suggested.

Her cheeks heated up, and I remembered how all of her skin pinked when she blushed. Especially that sweet, spankable ass. "We did too much," she murmured, too low for Hoot to hear.

"Well then," I whispered. "We must have hit on a good compromise because I don't think we did *nearly* enough."

The Escalade started, Hoot still chuckling to himself. I wondered if he *could* hear our conversation.

McKenzie stared at me. "You said we could do more later!"

"And trust me, we will," I replied. I stroked my hand over her thigh and made her shiver. Her body was so wonderfully responsive.

She swatted my hand. "You're not playing fair."

"All's fair in love and war," I said. It took a moment for the phrase to sink in between us, turning into something we hadn't even spoken about yet.

"Um…" She was blushing again.

I wanted to tell Hoot to turn around and leave us in that motel room until we'd worked out every single kink of our relationship, in bed and out. Instead, I squeezed her knee. "We're going to get there. I'm sure you know where this is going."

Her breath hitched. "Will, I don't… it's too soon… I'm not sure…"

I leaned in and gave her a toe-curling kiss. "I know. Me, too. But it's something I'd like to leave on the table."

"Table this for later?" she murmured, remembering my earlier words.

"Exactly." I settled back and patted my shoulder. "Now, come on. I know you must be tired."

She rolled her eyes. "And whose fault is that?"

"Mine," I responded unrepentantly.

Hoot snickered, and she blushed again before squeezing her eyes shut and laying her head on my shoulder.

I kissed her hair and put an arm around her, cuddling her into my side.

"Y'all are very lucky you like each other. This'd be a long trip if y'all didn't," Hoot said.

"True." I frowned at the back of Hoot's scraggly head. "Say, Hoot? It occurs to me we know so little about you…"

"And we're gonna keep it that way." He seemed immovable.

Still, I had to push my luck. "Yes, but we're—"

"*And we're gonna keep it that way*," he repeated icily.

I closed my mouth. "Yes, sir."

Hoot snorted. "Ain't nobody 'sir'd' me in a hunnert years."

"They should. It's a sign of respect," I said.

Hoot burst out laughing. "Hoot's just fine, son. Do they 'sir' you at work? Reckon they do."

"True. But they don't really mean it. I'm window dressing. Or I was. Now I'm a threat, I guess. My grandfather seems to be treating this very seriously, anyway," I replied.

"Damn skippy, you're a threat. And let me tell you somethin'. When you're starin' that bastard down in court, you remember ol' Hoot told you to be brave. Cuz ain't nothin' more intimidatin' than havin' to rat out your family." He shook his head. "'Course I wouldn't exactly put it that way. When you get there, y'all will be doin' the world a heap o'good."

"I hope so. I just worry I'll take down my grandfather only to have this Ibrahim or sheik or whoever step right in and take over where he left off," I muttered.

"Could be. But y'all ain't involved with Ibra-whose-it or the sheik. That's somethin' for McKenzie's parents to work out," he said.

I grimaced. "And then that weed gets pulled, and six spring up in its place. It must feel like Sisyphus working in law enforcement."

"That ol' bastard pushin' the rock up the hill?" he inquired, and I nodded. He shrugged. "Gotta pull them weeds, or they get all overgrown like crabgrass. All anyone can do is try."

"I suppose that's true." I looked down at the sleeping McKenzie and smoothed her hair back from her face, tucking it behind her ear. "Maybe I can free us, at least."

"Tall order, but I'm rootin' for you," he said.

"Thanks," I replied.

* * *

I didn't realize I'd fallen asleep until Hoot hit some rumble strips.

"Tarnation," he grunted, pulling the Escalade back into the lane. "It's cuz this big boat here is takin' up too much of the road!"

McKenzie let out a little snort but kept sleeping. I really had tired her out. "I don't suppose you'll tell us where we're headed, Hoot?"

"Sure won't. But I'll tell you who we're headed to," he responded.

That was more than he'd ever offered up before. "Who?" I asked.

"While y'all were playing hide-the-cucumber last night, I found McKenzie's grandparents," he said proudly.

My stomach roiled. "Did we really want to find them?" I hazarded.

"I know what your opinion of them is," he replied. "But they're McKenzie's family, and they're in danger, too. And, I'm sure you know, last time they were in danger, Hank lost his legs."

"He got them back," I pointed out. "He didn't lose his legs, just his ability to walk on them."

"If we're splittin' hairs here..." he muttered.

"They're not good people," I reiterated from our earlier conversation.

Hoot shrugged. "People change. And family's family."

I sighed and stared at the ceiling. "I'm not going to change your mind, am I?"

"Nope," he said.

"Fine." I gave in. "But I want to make sure we have an exit strategy that includes dropping them somewhere safe and getting the hell out of Dodge because I don't want them trash-talking McKenzie's parents and upsetting her."

He raised an eyebrow at me in the rearview mirror. "Son, you gotta be dumber'n dog shit if you're thinkin' they ain't already got somethin' to complain about without bringin' Caleb and Jacey into it."

"What would that be?" I asked, confused.

"Y'all came outta the same hoo-ha, now didn't y'all?" he said. "They'll know that."

I felt my cheeks heat up. "We already worked that out."

"Y'all did. They didn't," he replied.

He had a point. I groaned and squeezed my eyes shut. "Why are we going to rescue them again?"

"Family's family," he said again. "Don't nothin' change that."

McKenzie shifted, and I knew she was waking up. She made the same cute little snuffling sound she did when we were in bed together. "We there yet?" she yawned, blinking awake.

"Got us another ten hours at least," Hoot responded. "Dependin' on traffic."

"Will we need to stop for the night again?" she asked, looking outside at the setting sun.

Hoot looked out the windshield and hemmed and hawed a bit before saying, "I reckon so. I ain't givin' Will here our destination, and I ain't as young as I used to be. I don't fancy drivin' through the night."

"I could drive," she muttered.

"Ain't givin' you the location, either," he replied firmly.

I decided to bite the bullet right then, though I loathed bringing up the issue we'd just resolved. "So… we're going to go rescue your grandparents and your uncle."

"Sam," Hoot provided. "Boy's name is Sam. 'Bout thirty-one, so your age, then."

That was just going to make things more awkward. I was sure of it. "So, your Uncle Sam… okay, that just sounded wrong. It makes him sound like the IRS or something."

He chuckled. "Sure does."

"I thought you said they're bad people?" she asked hesitantly.

"They are. But Hoot says—"

"Family's family," he repeated.

"Oh." Her brow creased in the cutest way right between her

eyebrows, and it made me want to kiss the spot, but I didn't want to interrupt her thought process. "So… we're going to go save them."

Hoot nodded. "That's right."

"Even though they're probably going to hate us?" she went on.

"Even though," he agreed.

She'd come to the same conclusion Hoot had brought me to without any outside help. Smart as a whip was my honeybee. "Look, we're not related. We were born eleven years apart. Your mother was my surrogate. That's all. She is *your* mom. We didn't do anything creepy like grow up together…"

"My parents aren't creepy!" she snapped.

Shit. "I didn't mean it that way. Besides, they met when they were teenagers. It wasn't as though they were ever really brother and sister," I backpedaled quickly.

McKenzie's jaw jutted out mutinously, but then she sighed. "Fine, okay. I know you didn't mean it that way."

"Thank you," I sighed with relief. "I'm just saying…"

"You're trying to make sure I don't have second thoughts again," she said.

I rubbed the back of my neck. "Okay, yes. A bit. But I'm also formulating the argument I'm going to be using on your grandfather. Whether it will penetrate his thick skull or not, I don't know."

"We'll just pretend not to be together in front of them," she decided. "Easy."

I gaped at her. "Easy? How is that 'easy'?!"

"I'm with Will on that one. Couples got their ways about 'em. Y'all lean into each other, laugh at each other's jokes in a special way. Y'all got a look in your eye," Hoot said.

"Oh." She looked puzzled. "I suppose there is that. We can try?"

"It didn't work out so well for your parents," I reminded her. "That motherfucker."

McKenzie squared her shoulders. "Then we'll just have to be completely upfront with them. Get it right out there in the open. That means they won't be surprised later."

"If he hits you, honeybee, I'm going to kill him," I said flatly.

"Get in line, son," Hoot chimed in. "Nah, I'll make sure they know my help's conditional. Ain't gonna be no fightin' in my truck."

I thought for a beat then responded, "Good plan."

"Besides, could be they want to meet their granddaughter," he said.

I doubted that. I doubted that very much.

15

UP ALL NIGHT

McKenzie

I wasn't so sure my grandparents were going to be happy to meet me. From what Will said, it didn't seem like they'd been too sad to lose my parents, and as far as I knew, they hadn't tried to contact us in all these years. That was about thirty years for my parents and all nineteen years of my life.

We stopped at another motel at nightfall, this one even seedier than the last one, and Hoot got us rooms that were right next to each other.

Will made a face when he took our key. "It's sticky."

"Don't ask too many questions. Reckon y'all don't want to know," Hoot advised us.

Will gingerly opened our door. Or at least tried to. Aside from nearly having to break the key to unlock it, he had to put his shoulder to the warped wood for it to pop open.

Inside, aside from cigarette burns… everywhere… it appeared to be mostly clean. I was afraid to check the bathroom.

Will did it on our behalf after shoving the door closed and locking it behind us. "I don't want you running into anything gross."

"I'll let you hero your way through this one, thanks," I said.

He went into the bathroom, and I heard some rustling for a moment, then he came back out with a stiff face. "It's clean. Don't spend too much time poking through the trash, though."

"Why?" I asked.

"You know those things we don't need?" he replied.

I thought for a moment, then made a face. "Condoms?"

"Yes. Someone needed them pretty badly." He shuddered. "Thank God for Kleenex. Or whatever sandpaper they're calling tissue in there."

"Ugh. Okay, not questioning the trash," I said.

"I shoved a few tissues on top just for good measure," he added. "But still, like Hoot said, 'Don't ask too many questions.'"

"Thank you," I replied and hugged him. I rested my ear on his chest and heard his steady heartbeat. I hadn't realized what a bundle of nerves I was until I heard the calming thump-thump of his heart.

Will combed his fingers through my hair. "I'm going to make sure nothing bad happens to you when we meet your grandparents, okay?"

"Don't punch my grandpa just for firing off his mouth, though. There should be levels of escalation here," I advised him.

"Level 1: Shut the FUCK up?" he teased.

"You think I'm kidding around, but I'm not." I looked up at him. "I think I'd like to at least *try* with them. Like Hoot said, they are my family."

He cupped my cheek and ran his thumb along my cheekbone. "Whatever you want, honeybee. I'll follow your lead. I'll try, anyway. But if he hits you, he's a dead man."

"Okay." I figured I had to agree to that one. Besides, Hoot would probably get to him first, and I knew that man was a stone-cold killer.

"So." He lowered his hand to my breast, thumbing my sensitive nipple through my shirt. "Should we 'practice' some more for the 'big game'?"

I groaned and laughed into his sweater even while my loins began to tingle. "You do know, last night, I was thinking about it like training for the Olympics, don't you?"

Will grinned. "I do now. I know you're going to get gold in the pole vault, don't worry."

"Oh my God." I laughed harder. "Can we use any more euphemisms?"

"I know a few dozen. Let's see here… do you think we'll play hide-the-salami tonight?" he teased.

"Depends on whether or not the coach thinks I'm ready, doesn't it?" I said.

"A good coach also listens to the athletes to see if *they* think they're ready," he replied.

I still felt sore. "I… honestly don't know, Coach."

He gave me a long, slow kiss. "We don't have to decide that tonight, either."

I smiled with relief. Then I quirked an eyebrow at him. "You know," I said, "I still haven't sucked your dick."

Will swallowed. "We'd best remedy that."

"I thought so, too." I slid my hands down his front and opened his pants.

"Honeybee, you are evidence that Jesus loves me and wants me to be happy," he groaned when I pushed his pants and boxers down, revealing his semi-hard length, which was still pretty intimidating. He kicked off his shoes and swept his clothes aside.

He was taking off his shirt when I knelt down and wrapped my hand as far as it would go around his thick base. He froze. "Jesus, woman, give a man a chance!"

"No," I replied cheekily and pressed my lips over his fat head.

Will's sweater and undershirt dropped to the floor to pile on top of his other clothes. His cock swelled even more, and I thought I'd have to unhinge my jaw just to get the head of him in my mouth.

"You're doing great," he encouraged and that boosted my morale enough to try. I was afraid I'd get him with my teeth, though, so I started licking him instead, then shuffled my hand over his wet shaft.

He didn't seem to mind. His hips moved back and forth, and he buried his hand in my hair, panting.

"You are seriously big," I told him, licking precum off the head of his cock. "I don't know if I can get you in my mouth."

"Don't worry about it," he responded, his voice strained. "Just keep doing what you're doing."

I kept stroking and licking, sucking around his dripping tip, widening my lips as much as I could without grazing him.

Then he was coming down my throat, groaning with his release.

I swallowed, and kept swallowing, until he finished.

"Clothes. Off. Now," he said once his cock had returned to… okay, he still had a semi.

Wow.

Would he ever get tired? Once we were fully intimate, just how long would he be able to go? Would I be able to keep up?!

"If you keep staring at it, I'm going to get hard again," he warned.

I looked up, my eyes wide. "You're still hard anyway!"

"Not completely. Now. Clothes. Off." His lip pulled up at the corner, his smile softening his barked order.

"You're lucky you're hot," I fake-grumbled, standing and pulling off my clothes.

Will watched the whole process, so I gave him a little shimmy for good measure. He licked his lips, and suddenly, my inner muscles were quivering with anticipation.

"You like that, honeybee?" he murmured as I stepped out of my jeans and underwear. "You thinking about my tongue?"

"Maaaaaybe," I replied, trying to be coy. But then I tripped over the waistband of my underwear and landed on the bed with a rather undignified plop.

"I think so." He loomed over me, and my clumsiness did not seem to have diminished his lust one bit. "I think I need another taste of that sweet, sweet honey."

I spread my legs. I didn't care if that made me look easy. This was Will. As far as I was concerned, for him, I could be easy. Very easy.

He swallowed, looking down at my splayed sex. "You're already so wet."

"Your fault," I accused him. "You're too hot for your own good."

"I think I'm gonna have to use the tip tonight," he whispered.

My eyebrows hit my hairline. "You think you'll be satisfied with just the tip?"

"I'm going to have to be. I'd satisfy you for days, if I could, but Hoot's going to want to get back on the road in the morning," he responded mournfully.

"True." I spread my legs wider when he moved over me, willing to accept the tip, or whatever he was going to give me, whether it was painful or not. I was getting impatient to be one with him. It was a lusty frustration that was going to drive me crazy within the next few days if he didn't fuck me properly.

Will reached down, grazing his fingers over my belly before cupping my sex. He pushed two, then three, fingers inside. The fourth just didn't make it, and I let out a sound of frustration.

"It's okay. We'll get this down, don't worry," he said calmly.

"How can you be so patient?!" I all but whined.

"I'm eleven years older than you. Things don't always seem so urgent when you get older," he explained.

I looked down and saw his cock was at full attention, straining and dribbling precum on my leg. "Uh-huh. Big boy there seems to think it's pretty urgent."

"Big boy isn't the brains of the operation." He chuckled, doing something so delicious with his fingers that my eyes rolled back in my head, and I came apart around him.

Will pulled his fingers back and licked them one by one, locking eyes with me.

I made a sound akin to an animal begging for food.

"Just the tip," he said again, lining himself up with my entrance.

I didn't think he could hold back. No man could possibly have that kind of self-restraint. So I took a deep breath and braced myself...

... for just the tip.

Blinking in surprise, I almost didn't feel the slight burn as he used three inches of his impressive length—max—to thrust carefully in and out.

"Are you okay?" he asked between his teeth.

The effort must have cost him immensely. "You can, you know, try more of you. Inside."

His laugh was strained. "Not yet. Another night. I've barely loosened you up properly." He kept going.

Just the tip was still enough to hit just the right place inside me, and I clutched his shoulders, digging my nails in as pleasure built.

"Bad kitty," he joked, though it took effort. He kept going until I came again.

It felt so good I didn't even realize I'd scratched my nails down his back.

Will grunted and then filled me with his hot cum.

I flopped back on the bed, panting while he played with my breasts and nipples as I came down. He drew my orgasm out for as long as he could, and I could have kissed him for it.

In fact, I did, surging up to wrap my arms around his neck and crushing my lips to his.

I felt a warm, wet trickle on my arm and looked down. "Oh my God, I scratched you!"

"Yes, you did," he admonished me in a teasing tone. "Like I said, bad kitty."

Guilt overtook my good mood. "I'm sorry."

Will kissed me again. "Don't be. It's not the worst thing that ever happened to me during sex."

"Oh?" I frowned at him. "What's the worst thing?"

"I have a big dick," he said, but it was without bragging. It was just a fact.

"Yeah," I agreed. "There are whole harems of porn stars you could scare with that thing."

He chuckled. "Well," he said, booping my nose. "Some women see it as a kind of challenge. Mount Everest, if you will. Not all of them have succeeded. With their mouths."

My jaw dropped. "You've been bitten?"

"More than once. And that's all we need to say about my sexual history. Although…." He nipped my neck and I knew he left another mark.

"Hey!" I objected.

"You mark me, I mark you," he said.

I pursed my lips, thinking about that. "Yeah, okay. Fair."

He grinned and rolled onto his back, taking me with him, his tip sliding out from between my legs. "I think tomorrow will go fine," he murmured, surprising me with his insight.

Because as soon as my head was resting on his shoulder, the doubts came flooding back. "Really?"

"It will. Because I'll be there. And Hoot. But mostly me," he said.

I threaded my fingers through his, and our joined hands rested on his muscular abs. "I hope you're right. Oh, and Will?"

"Yes, honeybee?"

"Don't kill my grandfather," I urged him.

He shrugged. "Hopefully, he won't give me a reason to."

16
RESTRAINT

Will

Florida. We were in Florida. Specifically, Miami.

"You couldn't have told us we were going to Florida?" I asked Hoot.

"Not if I wanted y'all to stay safe if we got caught. Y'all and her family," he replied.

I sighed. I couldn't argue with his logic, I supposed. "Well, we're here now. Is this where Hank, Jeanie, and Sam live?"

"It's Greg, Mindy, and Sam now, but yeah," he said.

"I think I'll call him Hank," I decided.

McKenzie frowned at me. "Because that worked so well with my parents?"

I winced. "On second thought, I think I'll just let Hoot take the lead."

"There's usin' your noodle," he said.

"Can we also stop at a mall and get some more clothes? Much as I love scrubbing these with hotel soap…" I requested.

He shook his head. "Cameras."

"Great." I looked at McKenzie. "How are you feeling about all this?"

"Nervous," she admitted.

I took her hand and squeezed it. "Hoot and I will be there. Maybe Hank—or Greg, or whoever—won't be hateful. It could happen."

"You don't make it sound very likely," she responded nervously.

I shrugged. "I don't actually know the man. And like Hoot said, people change. Maybe he regrets driving away your parents."

She nodded slowly. "Yeah, I'm sure that has to be it. I mean, I'd feel terrible if I'd caused my daughter that much pain. He must regret it."

It took everything in me to give her a reassuring smile and agree, "Sure."

Hoot snorted. "You're a terrible liar, Will."

McKenzie wrinkled her nose. "You really are. But that's probably a good trait."

"Not in business. But I wanted to be a professional football player, so, I guess I wasn't focusing too much on my ability to sham people," I said.

"You've sure got the muscles for it," she murmured.

The lust in her tone made my dick twitch. She hadn't been able to take me yet, down her throat or up inside her wet pussy, but what we'd done last night was still, hands down, the best sex I'd had in a long time. My body would have happily dragged her into the very back of the Escalade and gone for a repeat, but my brain reminded me I might not get any for a while. That made me, and my dick, very sad.

Stupid Hank.

"What made you decide not to be a football player?" she asked.

It drew me out of my imagination where I was kicking Hank out of a moving car. "My grandfather. He wanted me to pursue business. He doesn't really like when things don't go his way."

"Oh. I'm sorry to hear that." She gave my hand a supportive squeeze.

"It is what it is. Maybe he's regretting not just letting me pursue football now. Now, I'm a threat."

"The second he realized you had a soul, he shoulda given up on havin' you go into the family business. But that's family for you. Always thinkin' they know what's right," Hoot said.

"And yet, we're going to go see Hank," I muttered.

He glared at me in the rearview mirror. "Just cuz they're assholes don't mean you leave 'em to die. Well, maybe your pawpaw, but he's burnin' the world."

"I don't know how I'd feel if he'd actually raised me, and I didn't just see him on visiting days," I admitted. "Maybe he would have succeeded in making me like him. Or at least I'd feel a lot worse about betraying him."

"You would have turned out just as you are," McKenzie insisted. "You just would have had a lot more fights."

"Probably," I agreed.

We fell silent while Hoot fought the busy Miami traffic. She and I were both tired and dozed in and out.

Finally, he turned down a very nondescript middle-class street where nondescript middle-class kids were playing in their yards, and older people were lounging outside on lawn chairs, watching.

I recognized Hank and Jeanie, sitting out in their lawn chairs, almost immediately. My grandfather had footage of them as well, after all. I think every time a squirrel pissed near the property a camera was activated.

I wondered how many hours of footage he'd watched of me and what I'd been doing at the time.

The thought made me shudder.

"You're going in with an open mind, aren't you?" McKenzie asked, frowning as Hoot parked the Escalade right in front of the Collins' house.

"I'll try," I said. "But… I was thinking of something kind of disturbing. It didn't even have to do with Hank and Jeanie."

"Oh?" she looked up at me expectantly.

"I was just… wondering how many hours of video my grandfather watched of me," I explained.

She made a face. "Oh, gross. You don't think he really did, do you? I mean, you weren't causing any trouble until recently."

"I'm pretty sure he did," I sighed.

McKenzie then shuddered as well. "Your grandfather is a freak!"

"Tell me about it," I grunted.

"Y'all done? Can we get this show on the road?" Hoot asked.

We looked up. I'd forgotten he was there. Hell, I'd barely remembered Hank and Jeanie were there. "Sorry. Yes."

He opened his door and hopped out.

McKenzie took a deep breath while Hank stood and eyed Hoot suspiciously as he approached. "I suppose we might as well get out, too."

"Probably a good plan." I opened the door and stepped out, holding a hand out to McKenzie.

"... Masterson," Hoot was saying as she took my hand and came out after me.

I put a steadying arm around her shoulders. Jeanie's eyes flicked to us, and a hand flew to her mouth.

Perhaps I looked like my grandfather? I'd always been told I took after my father, though, so I couldn't quite explain her reaction.

"You came here to tell us Masterson's on our tail? News flash, you old hick, he's always been looking for us. Hasn't found us yet," Hank said.

Charming.

Hoot didn't seem offended. Or, if he was, he hid it well. "He knows where y'all are. He's just waitin' on revenge 'till he gets outta prison. He was, anyhow. Now? Will *the Third* messed up his plans. He's goin' after everybody."

"Baby Will? What happened with him?" Hank asked, frowning.

I waved.

"You're Baby Will?" Hank said, looking me up and down.

"I'm thirty, just like Sam," I replied with annoyance. "It's been thirty years."

"And, what, you're here to tell me Caleb and Jacey are in trouble, too? They in the SUV? You can tell them to go *fuck* themse—" Hank began.

Jeanie made a strangled sound. "Greg, stop! Just stop. Can't you see they brought our granddaughter with them?!"

Hank dropped his gaze to McKenzie, who gave him a weak smile and a wave of her own.

"She's the spitting image of my Caleb," Jeanie went on, clutching her hands over her heart.

"She is not. She's all Jacey. Except for maybe the hair," Hank snorted.

Privately, from what little I'd seen of Caleb, I had to side with Hank. McKenzie's fair features and wonderfully curvy body had to come from her mother.

"Hi," McKenzie said tentatively. "I'm McKenzie."

"*Are* Jacey and Caleb in the truck and just trying to soften me up with my granddaughter?" Hank growled.

It was official. I knew I was going to be punching this man in the face before we parted ways. "I'm afraid we can't find them right now," I responded for all of us.

"Well, they're not here," Hank sniffed. "We'd never harbor those disgusting little traitors, would we, Mindy?"

Jeanie looked stricken. "I..."

Hank rolled his eyes. "That's what time will do. Make you go soft."

"They're our children," Jeanie said softly.

"They could have gotten us killed!" Hank barked. "And our son. Poor Sam. May he never know about all this bullshit."

"So... you don't want me to meet Uncle Sam?" McKenzie interjected.

Jeanie and Hank looked at her.

"Well, sweetie, you see..." Jeanie stuttered.

"No. That would be a terrible idea," Hank said gruffly.

I resisted the urge to roll back my sleeves and punch him right at that moment. It got even harder when I saw the crushed expression on McKenzie's face. "You're ashamed of me?" she whispered.

"I mean, not because of anything *you* did, sweetie..." Jeanie tried to placate her.

"You should never have been born. You were born out of *sin*," Hank said. "But like your grandma said, it's not your fault."

McKenzie swallowed hard, and a tear trickled down her cheek.

My hands balled into fists, and I took a step forward, but she put a hand on my chest. "No, Will."

I grit my teeth so hard I was sure I was going to crack a molar, but I did as I'd promised. I followed her lead.

"We can go now, Hoot," McKenzie said softly.

"Reckon we can. We done the best we could. If these idiots want to stay sittin' like fish in a barrel, ain't nothin' more we can do about it," Hoot replied. He gestured for us to get back in the Escalade.

"Wait!" Jeanie cried. "Please, don't just go. There's so much I want to ask, so much I want to know…."

McKenzie shook her head. "No you don't. Not really."

"We got to go to Sam now," Hoot murmured, low enough that Hank should not have heard a word.

But he did. "You leave our son alone," the hard-headed fool hissed.

"Wish I could, *Greg*, but it's his choice and his life. If he wants to save himself, I ain't gonna deny him the opportunity," Hoot said.

Hank drew himself to his full, seventy-eight-year-old beer-bellied height. "You listen here, you uneducated piece of trailer trash…."

"Greg." Jeanie stood and grabbed Hank's arm. "We're not going to be able to stop them. I think the best plan is to go with them and try to explain things to Sam."

Hank stared Hoot down, but Hoot was a stone cold killer. McKenzie and I both knew it. And I think, by the time the staring contest ended with Hank looking down and muttering at the ground, Hank did as well.

"I'll pack some things," Jeanie said, turning toward the house.

I heard the sound of an engine and the slow roll of tires. Just down the block, a black sedan with dark-tinted windows was crawling this way. When I looked at the windshield, the sedan suddenly sped up.

"Uh… Hoot?" I alerted him.

Hoot turned and saw the sedan as well. "No time. Everyone in the truck!"

Hank grabbed Jeanie's arm just as the sedan's passenger window rolled down, and the shooting started.

"Sonofa…" Hoot drew his gun and fired back while the rest of us hit the dirt.

It turned out, not only was Hoot a stone cold killer, but he was a crack shot. The windshield shattered and the sedan rolled right into a lamppost. Neighbors and children rushed for their doors, screaming, several with phones out and calling 911.

"GET IN THE TRUCK, DANGNABBIT!!!" Hoot screamed.

The passenger door of the sedan opened, but before the man in the suit could even get his bearings, Hoot shot him dead center in the forehead.

Jeanie shrieked and sobbed while Hank dragged her into the Escalade. I grabbed McKenzie and lifted her inside before she got her feet under her.

Hoot shot out the back passenger window as well, just for good measure, but the seat behind it was empty. He then put his gun back in a holster under his vest and got in the driver's seat.

"I think Will is getting more legroom than I am," Hank complained from behind McKenzie and me as Hoot tore down the residential street.

"Greg!" Jeanie bellowed.

We all looked at her, surprised by her authoritative tone.

"Yes, dear?" Hank asked, clearly startled and a bit scared of this new Jeanie.

"Shut *up*!" Jeanie ordered.

Hank swallowed. "Yes, dear."

17

SHUT UP, HANK

McKenzie

Hoot didn't need directions to Uncle Sam's apartment, much to Hank's disappointment. He'd probably wanted to lead Hoot off in another direction or off a cliff instead of to his son.

Hank.

I couldn't even think of him as my grandfather now. Not after the way he'd mouthed off about my parents and basically called me an abomination.

Jeanie was the same situation. There was no way I'd be calling her 'Grandma' anytime soon.

Will was a solid presence next to me, for whom I was very grateful. He didn't judge my parents, and he didn't think much of my grandparents. Maybe it made me a bad person, but I'd have happily left without them.

At least I'd been charitable enough to stop Will from punching Hank. But it would have been like dropping a boulder on a marshmallow.

Hoot drove through the apartment parking lot very slowly, no doubt looking for more black sedans. I was starting to think the people Will's grandfather had hired weren't all that smart. They kept showing up in the same cars. Like the black-tinted windows weren't a clue.

"I still think this is a bad idea," Hank groused behind me. "Sam doesn't know anything about this. He's got a perfectly normal life with a perfectly normal family."

"Just one that doesn't include me or my parents," I shot back.

Will had his arm around me and squeezed my shoulder.

Maybe I'd be the one punching Hank by the time we parted ways.

"Look. Like your grandma said, it's not your fault. But we did raise Sam a certain way. He's a good, God-fearing man, and I just don't think—" Hank continued.

"Hank, shut up," Will said. "You're just making it worse."

"Don't you tell me to 'shut up,' you disrespectful little twerp," Hank growled.

Will raised an eyebrow.

"Hank, Will could mess you up with his pinky finger," Hoot said. "You might just wanna watch your mouth. Okay, I ain't seein' any threats, so, we might as well go in. All of us. I ain't leavin' none of y'all here to get kidnapped and shot at."

I reached for my door handle.

"Will you hurry up already? We can't get out until you do," Hank complained some more.

"Hank, they're going as fast as they can," Jeanie sighed.

Hank harrumphed. "Not fast enough."

"I will go back there and pistol-whip you," Hoot warned.

Hank descended into grumbling under his breath.

I was so tempted to go as slowly as I possibly could. But Hoot was already hopping out and seemed to be in a hurry, so I hurried, too.

Will came out after me and was almost caught in the ass by Hank shoving the seat forward so he and Jeanie could get out.

"Two-oh-three," Hoot said with certainty.

Hank's face fell. He'd obviously been hoping Hoot didn't know the apartment number.

"He might not be home," Jeanie comforted him.

Hank brightened. "That's right. He might not be home."

"He's home," Hoot said when we got to the door.

"How do you know?" Hank asked.

Hoot pointed to the shadow under the door and then put a finger to his lips. "Sam?" he asked, drawing his gun and leaning back against the wall, gesturing for us to back up.

"Yeah?" came the reply. The reply from somewhere deeper in the apartment.

With a sigh, Hoot cocked his gun. "You've got five seconds to send the boy out, or I'm putin' one right in your dick. Understand?"

There was silence.

"Five..." Hoot began counting.

The door opened and a man who looked a lot like Jeanie stumbled out, his wrists duct taped in front of him. The area around his mouth was red as though tape had just been ripped off.

"That you, Hoot?" a voice from somewhere in the apartment asked while Hoot pushed Uncle Sam into Jeanie's waiting arms. Hank and Jeanie huddled over him protectively.

"Sure is," Hoot replied. "Gettin' mighty tired of killin' your patsies, Blair. Don't suppose you could give this contract up?"

"Money's damn good, but it isn't worth all the trouble," Blair replied. "My men are dropping like flies. If it's not you, then it's other groups wanting to claim the reward, thinking I'm in the way. Which I am, but they could at least be polite about it. This used to be a gentleman's game. May the best man win, and all that."

"Reckon it's all gone to shit," Hoot agreed. "That's why I gave it up. But I owed a friend."

"Really? Lucky friend," Blair said.

"Not really. He's dead tryin' to keep these bastards alive. Two of 'em I don't even like," Hoot responded.

"Shit, Hoot. I'm sorry. Good luck to you." Blair, a man about Hoot's age who still had a few curls of flaming red hair, stuck his head out the door. "Oh, and there's a bomb under your Escalade. Sorry. Didn't know it was you."

"Fair enough," Hoot drawled. "Be seein' you."

"Hope not," Blair chuckled. He tossed Hoot a set of keys, which Hoot deftly caught.

The two men nodded to each other, then Hoot herded us back down the stairs. The key fob led us to a beat up minivan. Hank made a face. "What about the Escalade?" he whined.

There was a loud explosion. Will tackled me to the ground and shielded me with his body while heat rolled over us.

"Figure we won't be usin' the Escalade anymore," Hoot said calmly. "Now get in the van."

Hank didn't argue this time. He pushed Jeanie and Sean into the van, this time taking the middle seat, forcing Will and me to crowd into the back.

Will didn't look particularly happy about this development, especially when Hank shifted the bench seat back so his knees were almost in his ears.

"Dad, what's going on?" Sam finally asked once Hoot had us out of the apartment parking lot, down the street, and back on the highway.

"It's hard to explain," Hank replied. "It'd be best if you don't ask questions."

"Ri-ight. That's not gonna happen, Dad. Who are these people? Why are we being chased by men with guns? Are you ex-Mafia or something?" Sam pressed.

"We most certainly are not!" Jeanie balked. "We would never do something terrible like that!"

"We're protected witnesses in the Witness Protection Program," Hank said proudly.

Hoot snorted and Sam frowned. "Is that not true, Dad?"

"It's true!" Jeanie emphasized. "It's absolutely true!"

"Why don't y'all tell your son which side you were witnessin' for?" Hoot asked with his usual delicacy.

I turned in my seat and looked over Will's arm, waiting for the red-faced Hank to expand on Hoot's point.

"Well, you need to understand, there were circumstances…" Hank stuttered.

"Yes. Circumstances. Mister... whoever you are... you're not being fair," Jeanie protested.

"Cuz y'all are fair types. While y'all's kids were bein' shot at, y'all lived in the lap of luxury, waitin' to discredit them as witnesses against a human trafficker. Do I got that about right, Will?" Hoot said.

"Sounds about right," Will agreed.

Hank turned purple with rage. "That man almost cost me my ability to walk! What was I supposed to do? Let him kill me?! My family?! My Sam?!"

"I seem to remember you also had a daughter, but didn't give much of a damn about what was going to happen to her," Will mused.

On some level, it was nice seeing Hank squirm while Sam's image of him shattered. It was clear on my uncle's face. But on another level, it did seem a bit unfair. Not that I knew a *lot* about the circumstances myself, but I did know they had to have been impossible.

"Look," I said slowly. "Why don't we just let it go? Ultimately, they must have testified for the right side if they became protected witnesses."

"Actually, *they* got discredited and went into WITSEC for their own safety, not because of anything heroic they did," Will responded.

"Okay, I'm gonna need you all to slow down," Sam said. "I have a sister?"

"And a brother. Well, half. Half-brother, half-sister," Hoot chimed in.

"A hermaphrodite?" Sam asked, confused.

Hank groaned. "Jesus, no. My daughter and your mother's son went and screwed each other."

"They love each other. They got married," I said defensively. "It's not any weirder than you marrying Jeanie. Mom was fifteen when they met. They didn't grow up together and they never saw each other as brother and sister. But you couldn't accept that they loved each other. You wrote them off, and you wrote me off. You didn't even tell Uncle Sam about them!"

"'Uncle Sam'?" Sam echoed. "Okay, so you're my niece?"

"Yes," everyone else in the minivan replied.

"So, my brother and my sister are step-siblings but it turned into something more, and they had a daughter, and that's you?" Sam clarified.

"You're right on track, son," Hoot said.

Sam looked at his parents. "You had some kind of problem with this?"

"It's gross. They're brother and sister!" Jeanie insisted.

"They're... really not, Mom," Sam responded. "You completely wrote off your kids because they fell in love?"

"When you say it like that..." Hank muttered.

"What other way is there to say it?" Sam asked. He let out a long breath then gave his parents an icy glare. "Well, since you're just going to disown me anyway, I figure I might as well tell you now. I'm gay."

Hank groaned and dropped his head into his hands.

"How will I ever have grandchildren?!" Jeanie wailed.

"I'm right here," I muttered while Will squeezed my shoulder again.

"Mindy, he's just confused," Hank sighed, patting her hand. "He'll get himself worked out, and we'll have plenty of grandchildren."

Sam shook his head. "Hey, is there room in the back there? I suddenly feel the need to move."

"You can climb on up here in the passenger seat next time we stop, son," Hoot said, sounding disgusted.

Hell, it *was* disgusting! My grandparents were completely awful people. I couldn't believe my parents had come from either of them. "You're confused," I defended my uncle. "You think everything needs to go your way when, in reality, you're making yourselves matter so little to the people who love you. In fact, after this, I don't ever want to see you again." I looked at Sam. "But Uncle Sam is welcome to visit anytime."

"Thanks... um..." Sam grimaced.

I realized none of us had been properly introduced to him. "I'm McKenzie. This is Will. The driver is Hoot."

"H-Hoot?" Sam bit his lip. I could tell he was trying not to laugh.

"Make fun of my name, boy. I dare you," Hoot growled.

Sam held up his hands. "Wouldn't dream of it."

"Good survival skills. Dunno which side of the family those could've come from, but you got 'em," Hoot said.

"Sam. I'm sure if we found you the right girl, everything would work out," Jeanie pleaded.

"You're delusional. Tell me we're stopping for gas soon, Hoot?" Sam asked.

"We're stoppin' for gas soon," Hoot replied. "In fact, I figure we might as well go on into that there station." He cranked the wheel, and I could have sworn we took the exit on two wheels. Cars honked at us, but Hoot ignored them.

"We're not bad parents," Jeanie said after the minivan stopped at a pump, and Sam practically bolted from the middle seat. "We're not."

"Y'all keep tellin' yourselves that," Hoot grunted.

I had to stifle a laugh when Will found the seat release lever and kicked Hank and Jeanie's bench seat forward. "You're not even good people. How could you be good parents?" he asked.

Jeanie burst into tears.

I tried to care. I tried very hard.

But I just couldn't.

18

A SPECIAL KIND OF PREJUDICE

Will

I hated Hank Collins with every fiber of my being, and Jeanie not a whole lot less. My arm stayed around McKenzie until she finally decided she needed to use the facilities at the gas station.

"I'll get you your chocolate, if they have it," I told her.

"And Dr. Pepper?" she asked hopefully.

"Is there any other kind of soda?" I replied with a soft smile.

When she was gone, I reluctantly turned to Hank and Jeanie. "Need something?" I grunted.

"She's being just awful," Jeanie sniffled.

My eye ticked. "I mean from the gas station. Not a therapist. Though you could both use one. A good one."

"Thanks for the opinion, son, but we're really not interested in what you think," Hank said. "Who do you think you are, anyway? Your grandpa is why we're all in this mess in the first place!"

"I somehow don't think my grandpa would care if Sam were gay, and he always thought Caleb and Jacey were cute together," I replied. "Not that I like to sing my grandpa's praises at all."

"How are we ever going to have grand—?" Jeanie began.

"If you start talking about how you don't already *have* a grandchild, I'm getting you both an enema to get your heads out of your asses," I snapped.

Jeanie stopped speaking.

"You can't talk to her like—!" Hank started in.

I shoved the bench seat out of the way so I could get to the minivan door, causing them both to squeal in surprise. "I'll be back. You can get your own damn food."

"Why you little—!"

I ignored Hank and went into the gas station. I couldn't find McKenzie's chocolate, but I got a bag of Snickers since I could already tell this was going to be a *long* ride, and chocolate would be necessary.

I was just pulling four Dr. Peppers out of the refrigerator case when McKenzie walked up behind me and wrapped her arms around my waist. She laid her cheek on my back, and I set the Dr. Peppers down so I could put my hands over hers. "It's going to be okay," I promised, though I hated to lie.

"Liar," McKenzie sighed. "But it's the thought that counts."

"I'm sorry we have to ride with them," I said. "I think Hoot's sorry, too."

"I like Uncle Sam," she replied. "Riding with him is okay."

I nodded. I tugged her arm so she came around in front of me, and I kissed her deeply, wrapping her in my strong arms. "I'm going to try my best to make it okay. How's that sound?"

"I know you will." She kissed me again.

"What the *fuck* is going on here?!" Hank bellowed.

Both of us looked up to see him standing in the gas station doorway.

Jeanie was right behind him and peeked around his shoulder to stare at us, a look of horror on her face. "Oh my God."

Hoot came up behind them and shoved them both inside. The two gas station attendants just stared at us all. "Reckon y'all wanna be caught on camera. Figure this'll make things easier for ya."

Hank turned beet red and turned on his heel, storming out.

Jeanie made a grossed-out face at us and walked around the perimeter of the store, keeping as much distance between us and her as possible, as though we were a pair of rattlesnakes. "I just need to get a few items," she said quietly.

"You do that." Hoot grunted. He walked with us as we finished gathering up the items we wanted, frowning at Jeanie the whole time.

Jeanie came to the counter just as we were finishing checking out. She looked as though she wanted to throw up. "Greg didn't leave his wallet…."

"Don't worry. I'll pay for you," I said icily. I bought her pile of things, things I was sure neither McKenzie nor I would touch, then put my hand on McKenzie's back and ushered her out in front of me, putting myself between her and Jeanie.

Of course, that put Hank in front of her, which was not part of my plan. He leaned against the side of the minivan, his lips turned down disapprovingly. "You're sleeping with my granddaughter, aren't you?"

It really wasn't a question. "Yes, he is," McKenzie replied before I could. "And I'm guessing you have a problem with that, now that I'm suddenly your 'granddaughter.'"

"You know your mother is his mother, right? You are even more awful than your parents! You are sleeping with your *actual* brother!" Hank yelled.

"More footage for Masterson. I imagine he's enjoying the hell out of this," Hoot muttered.

"Mom isn't his mom. We aren't related at all. She was just his surrogate, if you need to know. They did a DNA test and everything," McKenzie said defiantly, putting her hands on her hips.

"It's still disgusting," Jeanie added after a pause. "I mean, you both came from Jacey."

"Eleven years apart." McKenzie rolled her eyes. "And my parents *aren't* disgusting! *You're* disgusting!!!"

"I have to agree with McKenzie," Sam piped up from the front seat.

"Shut up, you fag!" Hank growled.

Sam balled his hands into fists, and I knew if he didn't punch his father, I was going to.

McKenzie beat both of us to it, however. She slapped Hank right across the face. "How *dare* you call Uncle Sam something so awful!"

"He told us himself that's what he is," Hank snarled, holding his jaw. He looked as though he might take a swing at McKenzie, his own hand balling into a fist.

I put McKenzie behind me and puffed up to my full muscular stature.

Hoot didn't bother with posturing. "You either get the *fuck* in the minivan and keep your goddamn trap shut for the rest of this ride, or I'm leavin' you and 'Mindy' here to rot." His voice was so cold I wouldn't have been surprised if Hank's balls froze off.

Hank hesitated, but at least his fists relaxed.

"I don't want to ride with them, Hoot," McKenzie said softly.

"I second," Sam put in his two cents.

"Motion carries, but we ain't got no choice," Hoot grumbled. "Family's family. For the rest of today."

Jeanie stiffened. "What about tomorrow?"

"Reckon I'll drop you two at the motel and leave without y'all in the mornin'," Hoot mused. "Now unless y'all want me to leave you here for Masterson to find, y'all better get in that minivan *right now*."

I helped McKenzie into the back quickly so Jeanie and Hank could get to their seats.

"It's not right," Jeanie murmured while Hank shook his head vigorously, glancing back at us while Hoot started the minivan. "It must be bad genes."

"Guess that's all on you, then," McKenzie responded with a scowl.

Jeanie shuddered and cuddled into Hank's side.

Hank was blessedly silent for the rest of the trip.

But then, so were we all.

Animosity made the air thick, almost unbreathable. Sam stared mutinously out the window. Jeanie and Hank kept glancing back at us with grimaces on their faces. And Hoot? Hoot just seemed to be done with the whole thing.

We stopped at a motel long after dark. I was sure Hoot stopped only because he couldn't keep his eyes open anymore. He wanted this over with more than any of us.

"Me and Sam'll share," Hoot said, getting three keys from the listing rental office. "McKenzie and Will, and Greg and Mindy." He began passing out the keys.

Hank snatched ours away. "*I'll* stay with Will, and McKenzie can stay with Jeanie."

I growled deep in my throat.

Hoot glowered at Hank in the flickering, dying outside lights of the motel. "I don't think you heard me properly. Will and McKenzie are roomin' together. That's what's happenin'. I didn't ask for your opinion."

"It's gross," Jeanie said, wrinkling her nose. "I mean, they're practically brother and sister."

"I get the feeling you've said that exact same thing before to a different couple," I replied with false sweetness. "Good thing that all turned out well in the end. For you."

"It did for them." McKenzie stealthily snatched our key from Hank. "They love each other very much. I only hope they're okay. Not that you care."

Jeanie burst into tears again. "Greg, *do* something!"

Hank hovered over McKenzie, who quickly tossed our key to me. "Listen here, you little bitch…"

That was it. That was the very moment I lost every ounce of grace I'd managed to muster for these people on McKenzie's behalf. I pulled McKenzie back, and, just as I was about to set her aside and knock the stuffing out of Hank, Hoot stormed over and gave Hank a punch to the gut.

I could tell what Hoot had done could have felled thirty men. Concentrated just on Hank? The beer-bellied, balding bastard went down like a sack of potatoes, groaning and holding his stomach.

"We done?" Hoot asked dangerously.

I nodded, even though his wrath wasn't even directed at me.

Hank managed a shaky wheeze while Jeanie knelt next to him and began to fuss.

"I'm takin' that as a 'yes,'" Hoot said. "Y'all go to your room when you can get him off the ground. Sam, you come with me. Will, McKenzie, y'all go to your room, too. I ain't gonna stand out here all night refereein' y'all." He began stomping in the direction of his room, Sam trotting behind.

I took McKenzie's hand, and we started toward our room, which was between Hank and Jeanie's, and Sam and Hoot's.

"Disgusting," Hank coughed as Jeanie got him to his feet.

I stiffened and started to turn back, but McKenzie tugged my arm. "Just let it go," she said. "Nothing will change their minds."

"True," I conceded. I still gave Hank a dangerous glare before sliding my arm around McKenzie and walking to our door.

After going inside, we stood for a long time in the dark, my arm around McKenzie. I could hear her sniffling and knew she was crying. But I also knew she didn't want me to know. Probably because I'd go tear her grandfather apart.

Which I'd have been happy to do.

Finally, I just wrapped both my arms around her and pulled her against me, cradling the back of her head and letting her tears soak into my sweater.

"I'm sorry your grandparents are such a disappointment," I said softly.

"They're not my grandparents," McKenzie replied wetly, but firmly. "No one that awful can possibly be related to me or my parents. I'm glad they never tried to find us. I'll bet my parents never tried to find them, either."

"I'll bet they did." I stroked her back. "Your parents are good people. They'd have wanted to know Hank and Jeanie were okay. And Sam."

"If there were any justice in the world, some court would have taken Sam away and given him to Mom and Dad," McKenzie whispered. Then she tilted her face up to look at me in the very low light coming through the curtains and cupped my cheek. "That goes for you, too."

I turned my head and kissed her palm. "I'm okay with how things turned out. I really am. I mean, not what my grandfather's doing, but... I'm glad I met you now. We wouldn't have turned out this way if we grew up together."

McKenzie nodded. "Will?" she asked tentatively.

"Yes, honeybee?" I replied.

She slid her hand down between us to press it against my cock, cupping me through my pants. "Put it in all the way tonight."

I groaned and pressed my forehead to hers. Just that one small action, small sentence, made me painfully erect. "You're sure, honeybee?"

"Yes," she said, and kissed me.

19

ALL IN

McKenzie

As usual, our kiss turned into something deeper, and the next thing I knew, I was lying on the bed, naked (after Will carefully inspected it, of course) with my legs spread and him between them, his mouth on my core, licking and sucking and doing sinful, sinful things I couldn't even describe. I wondered, briefly, if I should start sending thank-you cards to every woman he'd ever slept with for adding to his delicious experience.

Then I didn't wonder anything at all. I came hard, gripping his hair, holding him against me as I flooded his face with my juices.

"Honey," he murmured, kissing my thigh after lapping up everything. He licked his lips, staring up at me over my mound. "I'm going to put it in now."

"I know," I whispered.

"It's probably going to hurt a little the first few times," he went on. "Even though you're not a virgin."

"I know," I repeated. I spread my legs wider so his muscular hips could settle between them.

Will pinched and pulled my nipples, which sent delightful zings down to my core. I was still riding the last of my high when he lined himself up and pushed inside me.

He started with just the tip. My body accepted those first three inches willingly, remembering the pleasure from the night before. Even though I was still a little sore from our activities, I was also still warmed up and fairly loose from them.

'Fairly loose' did not, however, prepare me for the next two inches of his long, fat dick. I drew in a sharp breath.

Will stopped and let me breathe, caressing me as though I were the most precious thing in the world to him. He played with my breasts and backed off a bit inside me before pushing in again, but no deeper than before. "You're sure you want this?" he checked again.

"The... whole thing," I gasped. "Now. Do it now."

With a grunt, he took my hand and squeezed it before thrusting in hard.

My knuckles went white, I squeezed his hand so hard, and I cried out in pain.

"Oh, honeybee. I'm sorry. But I'm in," he whispered, kissing my knuckles. "See?"

Panting, I looked down and saw his pelvis was, indeed, flush to mine. I whimpered. "Hold me for a minute?" I asked, raising my arms.

He wrapped his arms around me and rolled us so we were each lying on our side, his hand squeezing my ass tightly so he wasn't dislodged.

I breathed through the throbbing ache, my body getting used to him. God, he was huge. No man had a right to be this huge. But, I did want to be able to take all of him. And this was the only way I was going to get used to it.

"Still hurt?" he asked sympathetically as he held me. He kissed my temple. "I hate that I hurt you."

"Your big dick hurt me, not you," I mumbled, pressing my body to his, my breasts rubbing against his chest. "I know you'd never hurt me on purpose. I want to be close this way. There was just no way around it, you know?"

"I know. I still feel bad," he whispered. He kissed me and nuzzled my ear, treating me carefully while my body continued to adjust to his.

"It probably won't mean a lot to you, but you feel so good around my cock, honeybee. So fucking tight." He sighed in my ear.

I groaned. "The only part that means a lot to me is that we can be fully together now."

Will nibbled the shell of my ear. "I'll bet I can still make you feel good. Maybe not fantastic tonight, but I can make you come a little."

"You can try," I grumbled, but kissed his neck in silent permission for him to do whatever he wanted. He might as well enjoy himself, even if I might not. Tonight.

God bless him, he was determined to try. He rolled me onto my back and kissed me slowly, fanning my arousal with quick flicks of his tongue. His hands massaged my breasts, then one drifted down to rub my clit.

I grunted when he pulled back a little and thrust deep again. It didn't hurt like the first time, but I was still sore. I did feel myself loosening up, though, which was a good thing.

"Okay, honeybee. I hear you," he murmured. He did it again, but much more carefully. He kept rubbing my clit and kissing me. "Wrap your legs around my waist."

I did, swallowing at the slightly altered angle. I hadn't been sure my body would be ready for it. As it turned out, it felt a little better.

"Better?" he asked.

I nodded.

He kissed me, then started thrusting in earnest. His dick rubbed against my clit on one side, his thumb on the other, and while my passage was unhappy, my body still tingled from that one point of contact.

"We'll go again after this," he panted, working hard to make me come. I was also sure he was determined *not* to come before I did. "Two, maybe three times."

I gaped at him. "Will, are you out of your m—!" Suddenly and unexpectedly, pleasure washed through my body, and I let out a cry, the end of which he captured with his mouth.

My inner muscles gripped his dick, and I felt the hot rush of his seed as he groaned against my lips. Every part of my body hummed like a tuning fork. I wanted this. I wanted him. And though I might be sore, I wanted it again. Just like he said. Two, maybe three times.

For some reason, tears formed in my eyes and dripped onto his shoulder as I held him tightly to me. We'd done something... truly... beautiful. I could feel it in my soul.

Will pulled my head back gently by my hair and kissed my tears. "Honeybee, did it hurt that much? I'm sorry. We don't have to—"

I gripped his hair much more roughly than he was holding mine. "Will Masterson, fuck me again," I ordered him, tears still leaking down my cheeks.

He blinked at me. "But you're crying."

"I'm crying because I liked it," I mumbled, kissing him. His lips tasted salty with my tears. "I want to be together like that again."

Will smiled softly and rubbed his thumb over my cheek. "I thought it was beautiful, too, honeybee."

"Good," I said, my cheeks coloring with embarrassment. I hadn't meant to get all emotional on him, after all. "Let's do it again."

He kissed me then rolled us so he was on his back, and I was straddling him.

"Holy crap!" I gasped as his still-hard dick pushed deeper inside me. It hadn't occurred to me that was even possible.

This angle was good, though, and after a wince of anticipated pain, I decided it wasn't too bad. Sore, but not too bad.

"Ride me, honeybee," he said throatily, taking my hands in his and threading his fingers through mine.

My ex, who Will had rightly implied was a terrible lover, had never invited me to do this before. I bit my lip and moved my hips back and forth a little.

"Your ex has a lot to answer for," he grunted. He brought my hands down to his chest, bracing my palms right over his nipples. Then he grabbed my hips and began teaching me how to move.

Soon, I found a rhythm we both liked. A lot.

"H-Holy shit," I gasped as I rode him right into another orgasm.

He filled me with his hot cum, shouting my name.

I collapsed on his chest, still so tight around his less-swollen dick that he didn't pop out. He trailed his fingers over my back, his chest rising and falling as steadily as his heartbeat.

Will was steady. And he was mine.

"Honeybee," he murmured into my hair. "I want to say things to you that it's too early to say."

I stroked my palm over his hard pec, dallying my fingertip over a nipple. He drew in a sharp breath. "That's okay. There isn't a timer on this. I get the feeling we're going to be together for a long time."

"Yes, I get that feeling, too. But, given the choice, I'd still choose to be here, with you," he said. He ran his fingers slowly through my hair, combing it against my back, over and over. "You're the only woman I've ever… wanted to think about a future with. Is that scary?"

"A little," I admitted. "Not too scary, though."

I felt him smile against the top of my head. "It's scary to me, too. But, like you said, not too scary."

He was starting to harden inside me, and I had to giggle. "You are insatiable, Will."

"Good thing we can sleep in the van," he teased. Only he really wasn't teasing, I found out, because he rolled me underneath him and slowly started thrusting inside me.

My sore body, nevertheless, accepted his big, fat dick. He belonged there now. He'd carved out a space for himself inside me.

And, if I was honest, he'd carved out a space in my heart as well.

20

A SPACE IN MY HEART

Will

McKenzie fell asleep against my shoulder almost the second we were inside the van. Hank glared at me like I was the antichrist, and I had a feeling he might have heard a bit of what we did through the paper-thin walls of the motel.

Good.

Not that I really wanted him hearing it or anything like that, but I damn well wanted him to accept it was going to happen. And keep happening. My dick twitched just thinking about tonight. McKenzie was right. When it came to her, I was completely insatiable.

"I hope you're proud of yourself," Hank gritted out as I stroked McKenzie's hair. My eyes were growing heavy but Hank's muttering kept me from sleep. "Defiling that little girl," he went on angrily.

I was, actually, rather proud of how many times I'd made McKenzie come last night, but I was getting very annoyed with Hank's vitriol. And it wasn't even 7:00 AM. "Wasn't Hoot going to leave you at the motel?"

"Hoot was. Then Hoot decided it might break McKenzie's little ol' heart," Hoot called from the front.

After our conversation the night before, I wasn't so sure it would have broken McKenzie's 'little ol' heart,' but I imagined after a while it would have eaten at her. I sighed. "Listen, not that it's any of your business, but I care about McKenzie very much. I don't want either of you to ever worry about that."

"What you're doing is wrong." Jeanie sniffled, and I was sure the wet rag was going to start crying again.

"Oh, stuff the attitude, Mom. You two have already lost three kids because of your little peanut minds. You want to lose your granddaughter, too?" Sam asked, turning around in the passenger seat to glare at his mother.

Hoot frowned at everyone. "Don't make me pull this van over."

He sounded so much like a dad giving kids a warning that I had to laugh.

"What's so damn funny?" Hank demanded.

"We are. Arguing like your opinion is actually going to matter to me," I said flatly.

Jeanie burst into tears.

"I know them big, fake crocodile tears've gotten you a lot of sympathy over the years, Jeanie," Hoot grunted. "But you're wastin' 'em on me."

"Me, too," Sam and I said together.

"You're all completely heartless and devoid of morals." Hank growled and put an arm around Jeanie.

"Devoid. That's a big word for you, Dad," Sam said.

Hoot smacked him upside the back of the head. "Stop stirrin' up trouble."

Sam rubbed the back of his head. "Fine. Sorry."

"Shouldn't you be apologizing to me?" Hank asked.

"Don't push your luck," Hoot replied. "Now, I think Will's plannin' to take a nap, and if y'all ain't got nothin' pleasant to say, I suggest y'all do the same."

I smiled and closed my eyes, leaning my head on top of McKenzie's. A good, long sleep would make the time go faster. I could already feel her tight, wet body sheathing my cock....

There was a loud bang, and McKenzie's and my heads knocked together as the minivan began to fishtail.

"What happened?!" Sam asked while Hoot swore and fought with the steering wheel.

"I'm hopin' just a flat tire," Hoot grunted, managing to wrangle the van toward the right shoulder.

A second loud bang put paid to any illusion I might have had about it being an accident.

"Tarnation!" Hoot managed to bring the van to a stop, but I knew we had two tires out now and only one spare.

Not to mention whatever trouble might be on our tail now.

"Stay in the van. Keep your heads down." Hoot drew his gun and stepped out of the vehicle.

"Will?" McKenzie asked anxiously as I ducked her head and mine down in the back seat.

"Something's wrong," I explained. "Let's just do what Hoot says."

I kept my head up just enough to see two cop cars pull up behind the minivan and the officers within drew weapons on Hoot.

"All right, old timer," one of them said. "We just want the five you're transporting. They're wanted for—"

"Please do an old man the courtesy of not lyin' to him. Y'all want the ransom," Hoot responded, sounding bored. "And if y'all know who I am, y'all know I ain't goin' down without a fight."

"Fair enough." The officer who was speaking took aim.

The officer's head exploded.

"FUCK!!!" the other officers yelled, taking cover behind their doors.

Hoot's gun was still smoking when he shot *through* a door and killed another one. I had no idea what kind of bullets he was using, but that door might as well have been a Kraft Single for all the good it did stopping a bullet.

"I've got to help," I whispered to McKenzie.

"Will, no!" she pleaded, gripping my arm. "You'll get yourself killed!"

"Yeah, I'm gonna have to ask you to just sit tight."

I looked up and found myself staring down the barrel of Sam's gun. "Sam, what the *fuck?!*"

"How much is your ransom?" he asked, his gaze cold.

"Sam, we're all family here," Jeanie gasped. "What are you doing?!"

"Family? Don't make me laugh. You've disowned everyone in this car, and I don't even know those two in the back," Sam snorted.

Hank, much to my complete and utter shock, put himself between Sam's gun and me. "Sam, you put that down right now. We can discuss this like men."

"Dead or alive, right?" Sam asked coldly.

I pressed my lips together, my hand slowly reaching behind me to the waistband of my pants.

"Sam! How can you even joke about shooting your f—!" Jeanie began.

Sam squeezed the trigger and blew a hole in Hank's chest. The lifeless man crumpled and landed on Jeanie, who screamed.

"God I'm glad I don't have to listen to that ass ever again." Sam grinned, and it made him look like a maniac. Something had snapped in his brain.

"Hank! *Hank!!!*" Jeanie shrieked, shaking the dead body and just causing viscera to get everywhere. His eyes were completely unseeing. There was nothing any of us could do.

"I suppose they still need to be able to identify you, though, if I'm going to get the ransom," Sam mused. "No matter. There's still fingerprints." He pointed his gun at Jeanie.

"Put it down!" I said, whipping my gun out and pointing it at Sam. "You stop this right now, Sam. I don't know what broke in your brain in the last ten minutes, but—"

Jeanie kept screaming, drowning out some of my words. Sam just rolled his eyes and blew his mother's head off.

I knew I couldn't hesitate. I pulled the trigger...

...but nothing happened.

"Safety, Will. The safety's still on," Sam explained. He turned his gun on me. "Also, drop it."

Fuck. I glowered at him and began lowering my weapon.

"No, no. Toss it up here." Sam gestured with his free hand.

With a low growl, I tossed my gun to the front of the car.

"That's better. Now, we can all be friends," Sam said. "I don't find you nearly as annoying as they were, so...."

While Sam's attention was on me, McKenzie, pale and shaking, snapped her gun out and fired, getting Sam right in the face.

The explosion of blood and mystery meat against the windows was spectacular.

"Oh God." McKenzie's hand shook, still pointing the gun at where Sam used to be. "Oh my God...."

"What in the *hell?!* I leave y'all alone for five minutes.... Whoa, there, McKenzie. You need to put that down," Hoot said, eyes widening as McKenzie's gun swung his way when he poked his head back in the driver's window.

"I shot him." Her voice quavered. "I-I shot my uncle. I shot Uncle Sam!"

"And I can't think of anyone more deservin' after what it looks like he did to his parents," Hoot replied. He carefully opened the driver's door, telegraphing his movements slowly. "You give that gun to ol' Hoot, okay?"

McKenzie shook, and I didn't think she was really grasping the situation. For sure she didn't even remember she had a gun in her hand.

"Honeybee," I said softly, holding out a hand. "Just give me the gun. Give me the gun. Then I can hold you, okay?"

Her lower lip quivered. "You promise?"

"I promise," I responded gently.

She slowly placed the gun in my hand, which I immediately passed to Hoot. I gathered her in my arms as Hoot put the safety back on and dumped it on the floor of the van.

"We've got to go," he said regretfully. "Damn, this is some shitshow here."

McKenzie sobbed into my shoulder. "I killed Uncle Sam."

"I know, but you saved my life," I told her, rubbing her back.

"We've got to go," Hoot repeated more firmly. "When we get

somewhere safe, y'all can do whatever you need to in order to get through this, but right now, we ain't got time."

I nodded and squeezed her arms. "Honeybee, we're not safe here. We need to go with Hoot," I said.

She didn't seem to be able to process that for a minute, but then nodded. "Okay. Okay, let's go with Hoot."

I pushed the middle bench forward so we could go out the less bloody side of the van and kept an arm around McKenzie while ushering her out of the vehicle.

Hoot grabbed both of us by the arm and tugged us toward the police cruisers.

"We're not seriously going to—?" I gaped.

"We ain't walkin'," he responded. "Get in the back. I'll get us somewhere we can switch cars."

I gently pushed McKenzie into the back of the squad car and slid in next to her. I could tell she didn't like the trapped feeling of the police cage being there and, frankly, neither did I. But I put my arms around her and whispered reassuring things I wasn't even tracking to calm her down.

Hoot got behind the wheel and pulled out into traffic, and we were off.

She snuggled into me, gripping my sweater for dear life. "I shot my uncle."

"Yes, honeybee. You did. But he was going to kill both of us," I said quietly, rubbing her as though trying to warm her up. She was shivering. "He killed your grandparents right in front of us. He wasn't going to have any problems killing us, too."

"I shot him," she whispered again.

I looked up at Hoot, who was concentrating on driving like a bat out of hell. Still, he spared me one tight-lipped glance in the rearview mirror. He didn't know what to do, either.

I tipped her tear-streaked face up and kissed her, pulling her into my lap. "It's going to be okay," I promised her. "Because I am going to make it okay."

"This is never going to be okay!" she all but wailed but clung to me just the same. "I... they... Uncle Sam... my grandparents...."

"Honeybee," I said in my most serious tone. "I'm going to make it okay."

McKenzie looked me in the eyes, and hers finally focused. She curled into me and buried her face in my neck. "Okay," she agreed trustingly.

I relaxed, and so did Hoot.

We sped down the highway, putting more and more distance between her dead family and us with every passing second. Exhaustion finally overtook her, which was a good thing, and she fell asleep in my arms.

"How you plannin' on makin' it okay?" Hoot asked quietly from the driver's seat, his eyes glued to the road as we weaved in and out of traffic.

"I don't know yet. But I'm going to do something," I said.

21

SHATTERED WORLD

McKenzie

When I woke up, we were in yet another car. This one was a sedan. My head rested in Will's lap, and he was stroking my hair and talking to Hoot.

"... she's going to be okay?" Will was asking anxiously.

"You're the one who promised her it was goin' to be okay. You said you're gonna make it okay. I'm guessin' it's on you now," Hoot replied.

I closed my eyes and snuggled closer into Will.

His hand paused on my hair. "Honeybee, are you awake?"

I decided it wouldn't really be fair to pretend to be asleep. "Yes."

"How are you feeling?" he asked cautiously.

Remembering the way Sam's head just exploded when I shot him made me retch in the back of my throat. "F-Fine," I lied while trying not to vomit.

Hoot pulled over to the side of the road and stopped the car. "If you're gonna throw up, do it outside the car."

I sat up slowly and nodded. I don't know how green I must have looked, though, because Hoot swore and Will immediately threw the door on my side open.

"Really, I'm f—" Bile bubbled up, and I just barely managed to get my head out the door before I puked on the ground.

"You don't need to prove nothin' to nobody, McKenzie," Hoot said once I stopped retching. He reached back and handed Will a napkin, which he used to dab my mouth when I finally righted myself. "You've done somethin' you never expected you'd have to. The first one's always the hardest."

"She won't be doing any more." Will hugged me despite the fact that I must have had dragon breath. "That was a one and done, desperate situation."

Hoot sighed. "Y'all might need to get comfortable with the fact that y'all will be doin' some more killin'."

Our heads snapped up, and we stared at Hoot. "Pardon?" Will said.

"I'm sayin' y'all are in some deep shit, and it's gonna be mighty dirty gettin' out of it," Hoot replied.

"I don't want McKenzie having to shoot anyone else," Will said defensively.

"You don't even know how to take the safety off a gun," Hoot grunted.

Will squared his shoulders. "Teach me. I'll do whatever needs to be done. She just had to shoot her own flesh and blood after watching her uncle kill her grandparents. I think that's plenty to give to the cause."

"Y'all are both gonna need to know how to do it," he said.

Will scowled. "I just don't think…."

"When it comes down to it, y'all won't have time to think. Y'all are gonna have to *act*," Hoot interrupted him.

I felt sick. "So… this is the way my life is going to be from now on?"

"Why did you think Jake was teachin' you how to shoot?" Hoot shook his head. "Wasn't for huntin' deer. Not with a handgun."

My shoulders slumped as he pulled back out onto the road. "I wasn't really thinking about why at the time."

"That was Jake. Always thinkin' ahead." I swore I saw Hoot wipe his eyes, but then he had his stern face on again. "Y'all are both gonna learn. You're gonna learn how to look a man dead in the eyes and deprive him of his life. Because if you don't, y'all are gonna get killed. I might not be around forever. Your parents got quite a body count around them tryin' to put that Masterson asshole in prison. No offense meant, Will."

"None taken. I think I'll take my wife's name, when the time comes," he grumbled, holding me gently in his arms.

The name 'Will Kent' snuck through my head. I tried to beat it back, but it kept sing-songing through my brain. It was so loud I blushed as though everyone could hear it.

Hoot gave me a knowing smile in the rearview mirror.

"It's not funny, Hoot," Will said. "We don't really want to shoot people."

"You want to live?" he asked, going serious again.

"Yes," Will grunted.

"Then you want to shoot people," Hoot concluded. "Trust me. Y'all can't be dependin' on law enforcement right now, as y'all saw. And a lotta good people have died and are probably still gonna die. So, to answer your question, McKenzie, you bet your boots this is how your life is now."

I groaned and pressed my forehead into Will's shoulder.

"Look, we're going to find a way to take down my grandfather once and for all," Will assured me. "And then your parents can handle that sheik who was never brought to justice. In the end, we're going to win."

"Ain't about winnin' or losin', Will. It's about survivin'," Hoot said.

I took several deep breaths. "When we get somewhere safe," I finally managed, squaring my shoulders. "I'll help you teach Will. And... I guess I can only hope I can look a man—or woman—dead in the face and shoot them." I bit my lip and looked up at Will. "I guess we found out I can do it for you."

"I could do it for you, too," Will murmured, bumping his forehead against mine.

"Long as the safety's off," Hoot reminded him.

Will sighed. "Yes, thank you, Hoot. I am an idiot."

"You won't be stayin' one, though," he responded. "And that's what counts."

* * *

We drove until Hoot's eyelids drooped. He pushed himself until nearly 2:00 in the morning before pulling off and getting us checked into a motel.

I was starting to get used to stale sheets and cigarette-melted pockmarks on polyester comforters with big eighties orange flower patterns on them.

Will inspected the place, as per usual, and found it to be passably clean. "Let's take a shower together," he said when he stepped out of the bathroom.

My spirits perked up a little, but only a little. I sat on the edge of the bed and looked at the floor rather than at him. "I don't know if I should."

"You don't know if you should what?" he asked, frowning. "Shower or shower with me?"

I felt chilled to my bones, my uncle's head exploding playing itself over and over inside my head. "I... I just... can't stop seeing it, Will."

"All the more reason to fuck until you can't think straight. It's a great temporary cure," he responded. He knelt in front of me and took my hands, meeting my eyes with his stunning blue ones. "Honeybee, you did everything right. What Sam did was wrong, and he was going to kill us, too. I know that doesn't offer a lot of comfort right now, and if I could, I would fly you on a private jet to Belize and pamper you until you felt better, no matter how many months or years that took. But right now, all I can give you is me."

Tears welled up in my eyes, and I leaned forward to wrap my arms around his neck, burying my face in his sweater. I sobbed without meaning to, but he didn't judge me. He just whispered sweet nothings in my ear and pulled me down into his lap so we were both on the floor.

I could feel his erection when he rocked me, but he didn't pressure me or even say anything about it. His hands rubbed up and down my back, massaging the base of my scalp and drawing circles near the bottom of my spine with his thumbs.

"Will?" I whispered.

"Yes?" he said, continuing to comfort me with his body.

"Make me forget. For a little while," I begged him.

"Okay, honeybee." He nuzzled my ear then brought his hands around from my back to my front, sliding them under my shirt. He cupped my breasts through my bra and rolled, pinched, and pulled on my nipples through the thin, silky fabric.

His attention sent delightful zings right to my core. I was wet even before he told me to lift my arms and took my shirt and bra off.

He dropped his head to suck on my naked breasts, and I instinctively ground against his erection, creating the friction we both wanted with my jeans.

"Honeybee," he breathed against my nipple, which pebbled. "I think we might end up fucking right here on the floor if you keep doing that."

"Then fuck me on the floor," I replied boldly, not letting up one bit.

Will groaned and slid his arm around my back, cradling my head as he lowered me to the floor. "You're going to be sore," he warned.

"I was going to be sore anyway," I reminded him with a teasing grin.

Still, after he pulled his sweater off, he bunched it carefully under my head, pillowing it against the floor.

I made grabby-grabby motions with my hands and he chuckled, leaning down while he opened my pants. "Want something?" he asked.

"Uh-huh." I smoothed my hands over his muscular chest, noticing how his nipples hardened under my touch. I pouted when he stood to pull my pants and panties off then take off his own jeans and boxers.

"Aw, did my honeybee lose her favorite toy?" He grinned as he knelt back down.

I opened my legs, cradling him between my knees.

He looked down at my aching core and swore, his dick straining, a bead of precum leaking out of the tip. "You are so damn beautiful." He leaned over me, bracing himself on one arm as he lowered his lips to mine.

I opened my mouth to take his tongue while his fingers pushed inside me, widening me for his ultimate entry. I ran my hands over him to my heart's content, my touch feasting on every tight muscle. Then I whimpered and arched into him as his fingers teased a powerful orgasm out of me.

"That's it, honeybee. Come for me," he whispered against my lips.

My whole body shook, and I felt sparks tingling over my skin from the roots of my hair to the tips of my toes as he rubbed my clit and finger-fucked me. I was still chasing stars when he gently removed his fingers and pressed the fat, wide, leaking head of himself against my core.

"I'm going in," he informed me, his voice tight with strain.

I giggled. "You make it sound like a military operation."

"Needs the same... delicacy..." he grunted, easing himself slowly into my tight body.

I wrapped my legs around his waist, pulling him deeper into me.

Will moaned and pressed his forehead against mine, panting. "Honeybee, we need to go slow now."

"I disagree," I replied, cupping his cheek and kissing him passionately. "I think I want your cock, and I want it now. I'm greedy that way."

He laughed, though it was still strained with the effort of holding himself back. "You won't be able to walk tomorrow if I'm not careful."

"Then you can carry me," I said.

With a low groan, Will gave in, giving my body exactly what it needed. His whole, long, thick dick.

It was a bit of a shock to the system, but it wasn't as though I hadn't climbed this mountain before. I wrapped my arms around his neck, pressing my whole body against his as he paused to let me get used to him again.

"Go ahead," I encouraged him, locking my ankles. "Ride me."

"God yes," he murmured and took my mouth hard while he took my body harder.

He was in me so deep, I could almost taste his precum. And every hard thrust just brought him deeper. I felt how he'd been holding back all this time, and, despite how sore I was and was going to be, I was glad I could give him his freedom.

His balls slapped against me as he pistoned inside me, and I dug my nails into his skin, hanging on for dear life. At first, my body complained about this rough usage, but when he reached down to rub my clit while he took me, everything in me got on the 'go-Will-go' train.

"I-I can't... *fuck*, honeybee, so... fucking hot..." he stuttered.

As he increased the pace and the savageness of our coupling, I knew what he meant. He couldn't hold back.

I didn't want him to.

I grabbed his hair and ground my lips against his, bucking my hips into every one of his powerful thrusts.

Will increased the pressure on my clit, and suddenly, I was in a universe of stars again, my raw center clamping around his dick as his cum began jetting into me.

It was perfect. So absolutely fucking perfect.

He groaned and held himself deep inside me, rubbing my clit until the last star disappeared. His dick gave one last twitch and we panted together, slowly absorbing what had just happened.

"Honeybee," he said hoarsely. "I'm so...."

"If you apologize for that fantastic sex, I am going to smack you," I told him.

Will let out a bark of laughter. "Okay, I won't then."

"Good." I framed his face with my hands and brought his lips to mine for a more slow, tender kiss.

"Mmm." He nipped my lower lip playfully. I already knew he wanted more, not just from experience, but because he hadn't completely lost his erection in me.

"You still want to shower together, don't you?" I asked almost desperately as memories of Uncle Sam's messy demise crept in from the edges of my mind.

"Yes. Then fuck again on every goddamn surface of this hovel," he informed me.

I swallowed. "I think I like that plan."

He remained still, however, and I frowned at him. "Will?"

"I don't want to pull out," he sighed with the cutest little pout.

With a small giggle, I nuzzled his ear and whispered, "Then don't. Have me again. Right here, right now."

"I like the way you think." He tugged my head back by my hair and feasted on my neck while rocking his hips against mine, his dick swelling more and more with every thrust.

I gave myself over to the sex. To the wonderful, mind-blowing sex.

Will was right. He was able to make me forget.

For a little while.

22
CARE

Will

I'd never fucked so hard or so often in so short a span, but I was a man on a mission. As long as I could keep McKenzie focused on her body, she wouldn't be in her head and thinking about the awful things that had happened the day before.

I was exhausted, mentally and physically, by the time we dragged ourselves out of our motel room the next day and headed to the blue Saturn Hoot had "acquired" while McKenzie was sleeping the day before. I was pretty sure, after seeing the chop shop, the Saturn was probably the result of ten different cars being cannibalized, but it had four wheels and ran and had enough room in the back for McKenzie to put her head in my lap and sleep, so it checked all my boxes.

"You gonna sleep, too?" Hoot asked as we pulled away from the motel.

"I should," I admitted. "But I want to be here if she wakes up."

He grunted his agreement. "You've got a way with her."

"I'm grateful for that today. I know she still feels bad about Sam. And we did witness her grandparents...."

"Mhm. Y'all are a bit green, but you've got it where it counts. I know you would've shot that bastard if the safety weren't on," he said.

"I would have. I tried to," I replied.

"I know you did. We'll just make sure you know about takin' the safety off next time." He glanced back and met my eyes. "Just sayin', this learnin' ain't gonna make you a thing like your pawpaw."

I winced. It had occurred to me that if I was able to coldly stare down the length of a gun and shoot a man, I might be more like my grandfather than I thought. "I hope not."

"You ain't shippin' folks in containers, lettin' 'em die and not carin'," he reminded me.

True. "I want to put a stop to all of that. But who are we going to be able to trust?" I asked. "How am I ever going to be able to give evidence in court if even law enforcement just wants to turn me in for the ransom?"

"I'm workin' on it." He stared out the window, deep in thought. "Gettin' people *to* court in one piece ain't really in my wheelhouse."

"I get the impression you were more on the other side of things," I hazarded.

Hoot nodded. "I was. If it weren't for Jake, I'd have been on your tail, too, back in my day. I'm retired now."

"What happened with Jake to make him so important to you?" I asked.

"Nah. That's a story I won't be tellin' you," he said quietly. "It's between me and Jake."

"Okay," I conceded. "I know he'll at least get a proper funeral. I'm sorry you have to miss it."

He shook his head sadly. "He ain't gettin' no funeral. I'll bet you my left nut them's who are after you took his body and disappeared it."

Shock washed over me, and it quickly turned to rage. "But he saved our lives."

"Life ain't fair, Will. Best you get used to it now," he said.

I swore. "I promise, Hoot. By the time this is over, I'll make sure everyone has a proper funeral. Including McKenzie's grandparents… and even Sam, I guess. I think he just snapped. It all got to be too much for him."

"I like how you give people grace. Even those who've wronged you." He pulled the car off the highway and took an exit. "Y'all are better than this life."

"There's not a whole lot we can do about it right now, like you said," I sighed. "Who are we going to trust besides you?"

"Don't trust anyone besides me," he said harshly. "Never trust anyone besides me."

I frowned slightly at the strength of his reply, but then, we were in dire straits. There wasn't anyone we could trust but him. "Are we going to find Jacey and Caleb?" I asked.

"Probably. That's the plan, anyway," he muttered. "Need to get all of y'all someplace safe."

"And Jake had no idea where they might have gone?" I pressed.

Hoot shrugged. "Might be he did; might be he didn't. He was more concerned about McKenzie. You're just a bonus."

"Well, thanks for taking me on," I said.

"You're welcome." He looked out at the road. When we stopped at a stoplight, he turned all the way around to look me dead in the eye. "If it comes down to you or McKenzie, though, you'd best know I'll leave you in the dust."

"I hope so," I responded just as fervently.

"Good." He turned back to watching the light.

McKenzie stirred in my lap. I prayed for her to go back to sleep, but instead, she blinked up at me, smiling in a carefree way. Then I watched it all come back. Her smile faded completely, and her eyes welled with tears.

"Hey, honeybee." I stroked her hair. "Do you want to sleep some more?"

"I don't think I can," she whispered. "I'm afraid of what I'll see."

"Did you have bad dreams?" I murmured sympathetically. I wasn't exactly keen on sleeping myself after what I'd seen.

She shook her head. "Not while I was laying in your lap."

"Good. Want to try it again? I'm still here. I'll still be here. I can watch over your dreams," I promised.

"No. But thank you." She sat up but still huddled into me, a faraway look in her eyes.

I put my arm around her and rubbed her shoulder and the back of her neck. "I'm here," I murmured.

McKenzie squeezed my thigh in acknowledgment. "Hoot?" she asked.

"Yeah, darlin'?" he replied.

"Are we stopping soon? I think I must have missed our last pit stop," she said awkwardly.

He nodded. "We'll be gettin' where we're goin' in the next half hour or so. Can you wait that long?"

She chewed her lip, and I was about to plead on her behalf when he turned at the next light and pulled into a gas station.

"Can't hurt to top up," he said. "Y'all go do your business."

"Thanks, Hoot." She hopped out of the car, and I followed her. I stood guard outside the bathroom while Hoot topped off our gas.

The whole thing went off without incident, or so I thought. She was in the bathroom for a long time, but finally the door opened. I held out my hand to McKenzie, but, to my shock, she yanked me into the one-stall bathroom with her, closed the door, and locked it.

"McKenzie?" I asked.

"I need you to make it go away again," she rasped. Her eyes were puffy and pink, her cheeks streaked with tears.

"Oh, honeybee, have you been crying?" I asked, laying my palm against her wet cheek.

She nodded and stepped toward me, pressing herself against me and wrapping her arms around my waist. "I need you to make it go away, Will."

I wrapped my arms around her and rocked her gently. "I'm not sure how to do that right now…."

"You know how to do that. Right now," she replied and stroked her hand over the front of my pants.

I hissed and Mr. Big was at immediate attention. "We shouldn't keep Hoot waiting. And this is a public restroom…."

"Please?" she begged me, starting to unzip my pants. I tilted her chin up to promise her we'd do it later, as many times as she wanted, but that here and now wasn't appropriate.

But when I looked into those green eyes welling with fresh tears, I couldn't deny her. "Okay. Okay, honeybee. We'll do it quickly." I put my hand over hers and helped her finish the job of opening my pants and scooping my rigid cock free of my boxers. "Pants and panties," I ordered her.

McKenzie toed off her tennis shoes and dropped her bottoms onto the edge of the sink. I guided her back against the wall in the small space next to the hand dryer. "I'm going to lift you. When I do, wrap your legs around my waist and hang on. I'm fucking you right here against the wall."

She nodded her understanding. I lifted her up and right down onto my cock. Taking my full length, all at once, without any foreplay made her gasp. Still, she wrapped her legs around my waist and her arms around my neck and clung to me.

"We'll do it better next time, but this has to be fast, honeybee," I managed to grit out before I began drilling her against the wall, fast and dirty. She started to cry out in pleasure and pain, but I swallowed her cry with my mouth, fusing my lips over hers.

There was no need for the rest of the gas station to know what we were doing.

I gripped her hips and rammed into her until I felt her tighten around my cock. Despite our less than ideal circumstances, McKenzie came with a cry against my lips.

Her orgasm brought on mine, and I pumped my cum into her, groaning.

I pulled out before either of us had fully recovered and grabbed a paper towel to clean McKenzie up before she put her panties and pants back on.

"Thank you," she whispered, tears replaced by a flush of passion on her cheeks.

"Don't thank me yet. I'll bet Hoot is not happily waiting for us right now," I said as I helped her back into her clothes.

She took my hand and squeezed it. "Hopefully, Hoot will understand."

I unlocked the bathroom door and glanced around. I didn't see Hoot, which was odd. I'd expected him to be tapping his foot right outside the door.

"No Hoot?" she asked, looking around as well.

"Not here," I said. I nodded to the bored cashier as we passed her and pushed open the gas station door, still searching for Hoot.

The Saturn was there, gas nozzle back on the pump, but there was no Hoot.

"I hope he's okay," McKenzie whispered.

It did feel like a whispering kind of moment. It was almost too quiet.

Then I heard Hoot talking around the side of the gas station. I put my finger to my lips, though I wasn't sure what instinct told me we needed to be quiet, and tugged McKenzie toward the icebox just at the corner of the store building itself.

"Yeah, I've got them. What do you take me for?" Hoot was saying to someone. There was a pause, then, "Well, I lost three of them because one of 'em went loopy, but we're lookin' for the Killeens right now. I'm gonna use the daughter as bait, of course. This ain't my first rodeo."

McKenzie's hand flew to her mouth, and she looked at me with wide, frightened eyes.

I frowned, hoping against hope that Hoot was just shooting the breeze with some other professional in the field. My brain provided the explanation that he had to keep up a tough front for us. *That has to be it.*

"No, I ain't bringin' 'em to you right now. I don't care if you got a jet waitin' in the hangar. I need the girl to get the parents, and I need Will to keep the girl. If you got problems with that, you shoulda hired someone else," Hoot continued.

McKenzie's expression said she felt betrayed, but I squeezed her hand reassuringly. This was all just some big misunderstanding. It had to be.

"Tarnation, Ibrahim, I ain't got the patience for that," Hoot snapped. "If you ain't got a bead on the Killeens, I don't know what to tell you. I did my part. You're gonna have to track 'em down and tell me where they are or there ain't a damn thing I can do for you. Not while I'm babysittin' these younguns."

My blood ran cold. Ibrahim.

I backed up slowly, taking McKenzie with me. I shook my head vigorously at her as a warning. Of course, my foot crunched down on an empty pop can.

"The... ah, hell's bells, Ibrahim, I think I been caught," Hoot said.

"Run!" I mouthed to McKenzie.

We ran.

23
HELL'S BELLS

McKenzie

I didn't even know where we were going, and I don't think Will did, either. But we had to go somewhere, so we just ran.

Will kept a hold of my hand, tugging me behind a gas truck and crouching down with me behind its back wheels.

"What are we going to—?" I whispered.

"Shh." He shielded me with his body and put a hand over my mouth.

I heard the scrape of boots on concrete, and I was sure it was Hoot. We didn't have guns anymore—we'd left them in the minivan. I wondered if that was all part of Hoot's master plan.

"Hey, lady, is this guy bothering you?" a thin man with a scruffy red beard and a baseball cap asked, coming around the side of the truck. He glared daggers at Will.

"He's coming," Will responded in a hiss. "Please, just go away."

The man took a step forward, rolling up his sleeves. "I'm gonna need you to take your hands off the lady."

"No, it's true," I insisted, waving at the man to keep his voice down. "There's someone after us…."

That made the man frown. Another scrape of boots made him turn around.

Hoot was standing there with a gun in his hand, pointed directly at the man's chest. "I suggest you git, and forget everythin' you just heard."

We're dead. We are so dead! my brain screamed.

Then I heard the deep cocking sound of a shotgun.

Hoot turned just in time to stare down the double-barrel hanging out the side window of the gas truck. A wiry woman with frizzy gray hair was just visible, leaning out of the window to point the gun at Hoot's head.

"I think you meant to wish my son a good day and back the fuck off," she sneered. Her hands were steady. I got the impression she'd have no trouble giving Hoot both barrels if he didn't do exactly what she said.

"You're right, missus. That was exactly what I was goin' to do," Hoot replied, raising his hands.

"And you were gonna give him a brand new gun," she said flatly.

Hoot handed his gun over to the red-bearded man.

"And the one you got strapped behind your back," the woman continued.

Hoot grimaced but did as he was told.

"And that ankle piece," she said.

With a growl of frustration, Hoot divested himself of a small revolver that was strapped to his boot.

Her son, meanwhile, was pointing Hoot's first gun at him, his hand just as steady as his mother's. "Man, you fucked with the wrong people today. Driving a gas rig is serious business. You know how much trouble we get?"

"I'll be on my way now," Hoot replied, backing away. "Y'all have a good day."

"Kneecap," the woman barked.

The red-bearded man didn't hesitate. He took aim at Hoot's kneecap and fired.

I'm not sure anyone but Will and I were expecting his leg to be blown clean off.

"Jesus, Mary, and Joseph, what kind of ammo you packing in this thing?!" the red-bearded man shouted.

Hoot hit the ground and groaned, blood spreading beneath him instantly.

"Shep, get in the truck," his mother ordered him. "You bring those two young things with you. We'll sort the rest out later, but right now, we've gotta be gone before the cops get here."

She said it so calmly, I wondered how many times she'd ended up in a situation like this.

"We can just be on our way." Will stood and grabbed for my hand again when I stood as well. "Thank you for—"

"That wasn't a question. Get in the damn cab," the woman snarled.

"Yes, ma'am." Will guided me up into the truck and into the cab behind the driver's and passenger seats, where there was a small space with a mattress.

Shep got in after us and fired up the truck. "Good thing we were done here anyway. Wouldn't want to lose this commission."

As the gas truck pulled out of the station, I wondered how everyone could be so calm. I was freaking out.

"You really can drop us just anywhere, ma'am," Will said. His voice was tight.

The woman turned around in her seat. "My name's Dolly. This is my son, Shep. Who might you two be?"

I swallowed hard and looked at Will.

"Oh, we're just—" He began spinning a lie.

"And don't lie to me. I've got a nose for it," Dolly warned.

"I'm McKenzie," I blurted while Will groaned. "This is Will. We're on the run from... well, the guy you just shot, but also a lot of other people. We didn't do anything wrong, I swear. In fact, we were trying to do the right thing. Well, Will and my parents were. I didn't even know about all of this until like a week ago. Has it been a week? I can't even keep track of time anymore—"

Dolly shook her head. "You, stop talking. You need to take some deep breaths and reduce whatever caffeine you're drinking by half." She turned to Will. "You. Explain."

Will squeezed his eyes shut. I was pretty sure he was angry with me, but these people had all the guns. This didn't seem like the best time to lie. "All right," he finally said. "This is a long story...." He calmly explained what had happened to bring us to this point.

"Human trafficking." Shep muttered it like a curse. "Mama, did you hear that?"

"I sure did." Dolly looked utterly disgusted. "And the arms dealing. And the drugs. And a whole host of other things. You're trying to testify against your grandpa?"

"Yes," Will sighed. "But everywhere I turn, I just run into more people who want to ransom us instead. No one seems to be interested in justice."

"Five-hundred-million dollars is a lot of money," Dolly said.

I felt the blood drain from my face. "Will didn't say anything about that."

"Of course he didn't. It's common knowledge. Everyone who's anyone from cops to cab drivers knows about the ransom. I didn't expect you'd fall into our laps, but, here you are." Dolly eyed us both. "Good-looking couple."

"Look, I don't have a lot of money right now, but I'm going to inherit..." Will began desperately.

"Son, we aren't going to turn you in," Shep said. "Are we, Mama?"

"Of course not. I can't stand human trafficking. Gives truckers a bad name, aside from the fact that it's morally reprehensible." Dolly sniffed. "I think there'd be less people willing to offer you up on a silver platter if they heard *why* there's a price on your heads."

Shep nodded. "Should I put it over the radio?"

"Nah. We need to spread it around more quietly. I don't want any more of those gun-toting sons of bitches on our tail," she said.

"We thought Hoot was a good guy," I explained softly.

"We don't have any idea who we can trust," Will sighed. "Even you, pardon me for saying so."

She shrugged. "I don't blame you one bit."

"How are we gonna get them to a good cop, Mama?" Shep asked. "It's not like we know many, and even fewer of them who couldn't be turned by that kind of money." There seemed to be extra weight behind his words.

Dolly made a sour face. "I am not calling your father."

"I don't know if we have a choice this time, Mama," Shep responded gravely. "I know you don't like him, and you like his wife even less…."

"What I like even less about his wife is that he didn't tell me he had one," she spat. Then she took a deep, bracing breath. "Fine. I'll call your father. You drive. We need to drop off the rig and get the truck if we're heading that far."

"Um… I hate to sound stupid, but I have no idea where we are or where we're headed," Will said.

"We're in South Carolina," Shep replied. "Dad's in Washington DC."

"And we're heading to him because…?" Will prompted.

Shep and Dolly looked at each other. Dolly grunted and folded her arms. "He's a judge. Some circuit or another. I'm sure he still has his eyes on the Supreme Court, but he's not there yet."

"You don't think he'll be tempted by the money?" I asked anxiously.

"He won't. That bleached-blonde bubble head he lives with wouldn't hesitate to get her talons into it, but Xavier's a good man. Except for the philandering," she grumbled.

"So… not exactly a safe choice," Will concluded.

She looked back at him. "You have any better ideas?"

Will sighed and shook his head. "No. I don't." He wrapped his arms around me and dropped his chin onto my shoulder.

Dolly raised an eyebrow at us. "Isn't he a bit old for you?"

I blushed but put my arms over Will's possessively. "It works for us."

She shrugged. "I guess that's what matters," she said dubiously. "But don't end up like me. I dated an older man once, too, and the only good thing that came out of it was Shep." She patted her son on the shoulder.

Shep grinned.

"I would never do that to her," Will protested.

"Uh-huh." She eyed him. "Well, I suppose we can only hope at this point. You've got her hook, line, and sinker."

My face must have gone scarlet because Shep chuckled, and Dolly sighed. "Boy, have you got it bad," she said.

"I… uh… um…" I stuttered.

Will's lips brushed over my temple. "It's okay, honeybee. It's still too soon."

I sagged with relief. "Right."

"'Honeybee,'" Shep chortled. "That's a new one."

"Here's to hoping. For the both of you," Dolly said. She faced front once more. "You'd best get some sleep back there. There's nothing much else to do while we go to get the truck."

"I'm not sleeping," Will insisted. "No offense, but I'm making sure we don't end up in my grandfather's clutches."

She nodded. "None taken. After what happened with that Hoot person, I'd be hesitant to trust anyone else, too."

"I can stay up," I said.

The other three frowned at me. "Go to sleep," they responded together.

With a frown, I opened my mouth to argue, but Will shook his head. "You can take second watch," he promised.

Something told me there wouldn't *be* a second watch, but I gave in with a sigh. "Fine, fine." I readjusted myself so I was lying with my head in Will's lap.

But I didn't sleep.

24

FAKING SLEEP

Will

If she thought she was being stealthy, McKenzie really needed to remember I'd been sleeping next to her for more than a week now. I bit back a smile as she faked breathing deeply and continued to stroke her hair as she laid in my lap.

"So, Shep, your father's a judge?" I said, trying to make conversation. "Xavier...?"

"Xavier Pope," Shep replied. "And we'll use that term 'father' loosely."

"I understand. I'd love to use the term 'grandfather' loosely as well," I grunted, thinking of William Masterson Sr. with no small amount of bitterness.

"Can do," Shep said.

Dolly shushed us both. "I'm trying to call the asshole. Would you mind quieting down for a minute? Yes, I'm talking about you, you lying, cheating, sonofabitch."

I winced, expecting Xavier Pope to just hang up, but she just rolled her eyes as he kept talking on the other end of the line.

"No, I don't need any money from you, thanks so much. Today's your lucky day. I'm about to drop a Supreme-Court-Justice-making opportunity on your doorstep. You just have to keep Felicity out of it. And I mean all the way out, or not only will you lose your opportunity, you're going to lose your balls because I *will* twist them right off," she snapped.

We all went silent. Even McKenzie held her breath.

"I have a young man here who says his name is Will Masterson *the Third*. And he's got quite a—did I stutter? I don't remember stuttering. Yes, Will Masterson the Third. Yeah, no shit he's got a price on his head. Of course, Milton's okay. You don't think I'd risk our son's life on purpose, do you?" she went on.

Shep cringed when his mother said 'Milton,' and I bit down hard on the inside of my cheek not to laugh at his predicament. If I'd been named Milton, I might have chosen Shep instead, too.

"They were on the run, and we picked them up. There might have been a small gun fight involved, but you know I always carry that shotgun. Can't be too careful when you're hauling gasoline." She pulled the phone away from her ear as Xavier started swearing so loudly McKenzie didn't bother to pretend to sleep anymore. "Well, I seem to remember *somebody* in this family being married—and still being married—to some hoity toity miss from the country club. If you wanted a choice in the matter, you sure went the wrong way about it."

Xavier stopped swearing, and she put the phone back to her ear. "That's better. Now, I've got Will, and I've got McKenzie Kent, who I guess is actually McKenzie Killeen? Her parents were in some kind of pseudo-witness-protection program." She paused. "Yes, as I understand, her father's name is Caleb. Mother by the name of Jocelyn... Jacey, yes. Hell, you seem to know more than I do."

Shep leaned closer to his mother to try to catch what Xavier was saying, just as I was doing the same, but I sat back again quickly when she swatted her son. "Eyes on the road, Shep."

"Yes, Mama," he replied sullenly and turned his attention back to driving.

"Of course, I call him 'Shep.' I can't believe you convinced me to name him after your father. Anyway, we're heading your way now as soon as we pick up the truck. I assume you'd rather we meet you at the office than at the mansion?" she asked with false sweetness.

Xavier muttered a response.

Dolly nodded. "Great," she said. "We'll bring lunch. I figure there's going to be a lot we need to talk about and very few people you can trust to even go get food, much less see to our wellbeing. I'm not an idiot, Xavier. I know this paints a target on all our backs."

I felt a sting of guilt. Like Caleb and Jacey before us, McKenzie and I, mostly I, were getting a lot of good people in trouble. Killed, even.

"Maybe we should—" I began.

"Just a second, Xavier. Will's about to try to fall on his sword or some other such stupid shit." She craned her head around and scowled at me. "Boy, don't make me come back there and slap the stupid out of you. We're just taking you as far as D.C. Once we've made sure you're in good hands, we'll be out of it. Don't you worry. I'm not in the business of getting us all killed."

I swallowed. "Yes, ma'am."

"Better." She went back to her call. "See you in about seven hours, Xavier. Make sure everything's ready." She hung up.

"Mama, you didn't threaten to kill him this time. I think that's progress," Shep grinned.

Dolly gave him a sour look. "I'm trying to sniff him out this time."

"I thought you said he wouldn't try to turn us in for the ransom?" McKenzie said suddenly.

"And I thought you were supposed to be sleeping," Dolly scolded her. With a sigh, she sat back and smoothed a hand over her untamed hair. "I did say that. And I don't think he will. But I also know he's still a human being. Human beings get tempted sometimes."

"I hope he's more interested in his career than hundreds of millions of dollars," I sighed. "It's a lot of money."

"Trust me, if there's anyone in the world who's in it for the glory more than he's in it for the money, it's Xavier Pope." Dolly tapped her fingers on her armrest. "Still, we're gonna be careful."

"We've been trying to be, but as you saw, it hasn't panned out very well for us," I muttered.

Dolly turned around and looked at me. "Chin up. Hopefully, this is the last turn on the merry-go-round for you."

"Hopefully," I agreed.

* * *

I finally got McKenzie to sleep for real by lying down beside her on the mattress in the back of the cab. I wasn't entirely sure she believed I would go to sleep. She probably just passed out from exhaustion. I had been giving her body quite a workout, and she was still struggling with the death of her uncle and her grandparents, I knew.

While she slept, I spooned her and held her against me, my eyes closed and my ears perked for any sign we might get double-crossed.

"You can quit with the act, Will," Shep said after a while. "You're a really bad fake-sleeper. Even worse than McKenzie."

I peeked my eyes open. "She's asleep now," I whispered.

"Good." Shep looked at Dolly. "Mama, you think she's gonna be okay?"

"I think they've got therapy in Witness Protection," she replied. "They must."

"I don't remember Witness Protection working out so well for Caleb and Jacey," I murmured. "Whatever Xavier does with us, it's going to have to be something better than that."

"Hmm. True." She tapped her fingers on her armrest again and opened her mouth to say something more, but Shep interrupted her.

"Mama, we're home," he said.

I carefully extricated my arm from under McKenzie and sat up, looking outside. There was a very nice-looking red truck sitting outside of an unassuming little home on an unassuming little street. The truck was the only way I was able to guess which house was theirs.

As we pulled up in front of the house, I saw my guess was correct.

"Okay. Everybody inside to shower. We've got two bathrooms, so it shouldn't take long," Dolly called, waking McKenzie up. "I figure you two have been in those clothes for a while now. Shep's sweats should fit you okay, Will, and I'll find something for McKenzie from my curvier days."

Dolly and Shep then got out of the truck, and we followed them out. I half expected a bomb to go off, a shot to be fired, a helicopter to descend from overhead, or something, but the neighborhood remained as sleepy as ever.

McKenzie took my hand, her fingers trembling, and I knew she was scared of the same things. I threaded my fingers through hers and squeezed her hand reassuringly.

Once inside the house, Dolly waved us toward her bedroom, which was the master bedroom with the master bath. "You two shower. I don't care if you do it together or separately, but you have to be quick about it. I don't like hanging around here too long."

"Feels safer to be on the road," Shep added from the living room.

Dolly gathered up some extra shampoo and soap from under the sink. "I'll go take a shower after Shep in his bathroom once I've got clothes laid out for you two. And if you're going to take a little intimate time, don't be too loud. No matter what we do, these walls never keep out too much noise. My biggest complaint about the neighborhood, but also one of the biggest selling points if you're on the run."

"You've been on the run before?" I asked while McKenzie poked her head in the shower.

Dolly shrugged. "Rich people always think they can have their own way."

Her cryptic answer just confused me more, but she was gone before I could ask any follow-up questions.

McKenzie came over to me and started stripping off my shirt. I let her. My cock knew we were going to be having intimate time before my brain had a chance to catch up. She unzipped my pants and went to her knees, but I tugged her back up by her shoulders, shaking my head. "No time," I reminded her softly.

I kicked off my pants and boxers after toeing off my shoes and socks. Then I stripped McKenzie naked and backed her into the small shower, closing the glass door behind us.

The water started out cold when it hit us, and I quickly turned us so it was pelting, freezing, against my back, shielding her from the unpleasant sensation. But it warmed up soon enough.

She kissed me with a desperation I wished I knew how to assuage with more than my body. I didn't know how to take the guilt and pain away, and that tore at my soul. I could certainly distract her, which I started to do by kissing her back and massaging her breasts. But I couldn't heal the pain.

"Will," she said achingly, and I held her tight, just letting the water wash over us for a while.

McKenzie was the one who grabbed the soap and started giving me a very, *very* indecent scrub.

I groaned, and my cock strained in her hand. I decided to return the favor, and soon, both of our hands were busy, and we were gasping with need.

She turned and pressed her palms against the shower wall, spreading her legs and offering herself to me.

Knowing she must still be quite sore, I gently guided myself into her and slowly pushed in to the hilt, biting my lip against another groan as I felt her tight and hot around my cock.

McKenzie whimpered, and I knew my guess was correct. I kissed her shoulder and her neck, massaging a breast and her clit while I thrust inside her. I wished we had more time. I wished we had a bed. I wished I could do something, anything, to make her burden lighter.

Instead, I could only do this.

She didn't seem to mind my failings, however. She pushed back into every thrust, taking me as deep as possible. I brought my hand up from her breast to her mouth when she began making loud noises of pleasure.

McKenzie cried out against my hand, and her inner muscles fisted around my cock. I had to bite down on my arm to keep a bellow of pleasure to myself as I spurted into her, letting her body milk every last drop of cum from me.

We stood there a moment, my cock still buried in her, warm water sliding over us. Then she crumpled in my arms, sobbing.

I held her tightly, then gently pulled out and turned her to face me so I could hold her properly. While she cried on my shoulder, I shampooed her hair. By the time I got to the conditioner, she'd pulled herself together enough to take the shampoo and wash my hair. We were gentle with each other, like either one of us could break at any moment.

She was still tearful when we got out of the shower, and I was patting her dry. I kissed her thoroughly, not knowing what else I could do.

McKenzie hugged herself against my wet body, and I wrapped my arms around her, stroking her back. I grabbed a brush off the counter and began combing out her hair. Wet, her hair turned an even darker, richer honey color.

"Stay with me, Will?" she finally rasped, her voice heavy with unshed tears.

"Forever and always, honeybee. You don't have to worry about that," I vowed, tilting her chin up so she could see how deeply I meant it.

She hiccuped and kissed me.

It might have been too soon to say more, but I certainly felt it. I was deeply, desperately in love with McKenzie Kent.

25

JUDGMENT

McKenzie

Shep had a nice truck, which meant Will and I weren't packed like sardines in the back. I still leaned against him, but at least Will's knees weren't in his ears.

"It'll be about another four hours," Dolly said, handing us sandwiches she'd made.

Along with the jeans and tank top she'd managed to find me, and the straining T-shirt and sweatpants she'd found for Will, Dolly had also gotten together a small cooler of food. While we'd offered to take it in the back by us, she insisted on having it at her feet. Now, she doled out food in a motherly way.

Shep crunched down on some Fritos, expertly navigating the road. If he'd been good with a rig, then he was magic with his truck, threading it through traffic like a needle. On the crowded I-95, we were still making good time.

Will and I ate ham-salad sandwiches and Fritos right along with Shep and Dolly. The drink of the day was Dr. Pepper, and I was grateful for even the smallest amount of caffeine.

"You could still have some trucker crack," Shep teased, shaking a bottle of caffeinated pills at me when I yawned.

"No thanks," I repeated while Shep laughed.

Dolly rolled her eyes. "I don't even let *him* have any most of the time. But we do need to get to D.C. in one piece, and it's been a while since any of us have slept."

"It's not going to make him jittery, is it?" Will asked cautiously.

Shep snorted. "Will, this is trucker crack. You don't think we'd use something that's going to give us the jitters while we're driving, do you?"

"Good point," Will conceded.

I put my hand on Will's thigh, and he blinked down at me. His arm tightened around me, and I nodded my approval. It was exactly what I'd wanted.

Well, a close second, anyway. Okay, maybe not a 'close' second, but it wasn't like we were going to have sex in the back of Shep's truck, especially right in front of Dolly and Shep. That would be… creepy. And disrespectful. And… creepy.

Will kissed my hair and tucked my head under his chin. I could feel his steady heartbeat, and it was almost hypnotic. I yawned again.

"I think Will's plenty alert for the both of you, McKenzie. You should go back to sleep," Dolly advised me. "Like I said, we've got another four hours on the road.

"I'm fine, thanks," I replied. The truth was, I didn't like what I saw when I closed my eyes, awake or asleep.

Will rubbed my arm. "It's okay, honeybee. I'm here," he whispered.

I shook my head vigorously. "Later," I mumbled back. "I just… can't now."

"Okay." I liked that he didn't push, just held me tighter still.

"Don't suffocate the poor thing," Dolly warned.

Will let up a bit, and I pouted. But Dolly was right. His embrace had started to get a little too tight. I knew it was because he was worried about me. I wished I didn't give him cause to worry, but then, *I* was worried about me, too, so there wasn't a whole lot I could do about that.

I'd killed my uncle.

And I could still see my dead grandparents.

I shuddered.

To his credit, Will didn't say anything stupid like, 'It's going to be all right.' He just kissed my hair again.

I liked that he didn't lie to me. And I liked that he gave himself to me fully. I never had to beg. Hell, I never even had to ask. He was just always there, a solid presence. The truth was, he could have used his money and run off to Borneo, leaving me in the dust. But he hadn't, and he wouldn't. Will had made it more than clear that we were in this together.

He also felt bad for starting the domino effect, I knew, no matter how clear it was that his grandfather would have had the upper hand if things had been left alone until Will Masterson Sr. got out of prison. Hoot had been right about that one thing. It was a shame he'd been working for the sheik the whole time.

"Will?" I asked after an hour had passed, and Dolly had dozed off.

"Yes, honeybee?" he responded, looking down at me.

"I'm glad you're here," I said.

He smiled and kissed my forehead. "I am, too."

"You two are good together. Don't let my mama make you feel bad about the age difference. I know a good couple when I see one," Shep commented, making me jump. I'd almost forgotten he was there!

"Thanks, Shep," Will chuckled.

As the scenery flew by, and the truck weaved easily between lanes, I started to get lulled to sleep despite myself. My eyelids drooped and finally drifted closed.

Instead of the carnage I was expecting to see, however, I just saw Will. Solid. Steady. Smiling.

It finally felt all right to sleep.

* * *

"We're here," Dolly said, and my head shot up, knocking into Will's chin.

He grunted, and I could hear from the roughness of it that he'd been sleeping, too.

I rubbed the top of my head, then kissed Will's chin. "Sorry."

"It's okay, honeybee." Will kissed the spot on my head I'd been rubbing.

We got out of the truck after Shep and Dolly. I saw we were parked in the parking lot of a large office building.

"So, definitely not the mansion, then," Will grinned.

"Definitely not. That's all we'd need, that witch riding her broom up to this situation," Dolly muttered.

Shep patted his mother on the shoulder. "Be nice, Mama. We've got to get him to help."

"Helping is in his best interest. I don't see why I need to be any nicer for him to have the brains God gave him to help himself," she grumbled but managed to plaster something resembling a smile on her face when an older version of Shep came out the door of the office building. Xavier Pope looked around him as though expecting sniper fire before scurrying over to us.

"Let's get inside," he said. "I dismissed Ms. Perkins for the day. It's just going to be us, for now."

Dolly frowned at him, but waved at us to follow and the five of us headed up to Xavier's office. I assumed Ms. Perkins was his assistant, and as the assistant's desk was empty, I decided my hunch was correct.

Xavier sat down behind his desk and gestured for the four of us to sit down in the half-circle of four chairs he had in front of his desk. I could tell from the divots in the carpeting that the setup was usually just two chairs. He'd thought ahead.

"Have you eaten?" Xavier asked.

Dolly plopped the cooler on Xavier's desk. "Help yourself." She took out more sandwiches, tuna salad this time, and passed them around to all of us, along with Doritos and Coca-Cola.

"Always prepared," Xavier chuckled.

"Sometimes prepared." Dolly smiled fondly at Shep. "Though I wouldn't change it for the world."

"Thanks, Mama," Shep smiled.

Xavier sniffed his sandwich before taking a tentative bite.

"I didn't poison it, if that's what you're wondering," Dolly growled. "You can't help us if you're dead."

"True." Xavier took a more aggressive bite then sat back in his chair. "You two are in quite a lot of trouble, you know."

"We've gotten that impression, yes," Will said dryly.

"A lot of people are after you. And you're in trouble for aiding and abetting an assassin who just killed five cops," Xavier explained.

I stared at him. "What?!"

"Relax. I know it was you in his clutches and not the other way around. I think most sane law enforcement officers know that. It's just that they're looking for someone to pay for the murders, and you're alive and 'Hoot' isn't," Xavier said, gesturing idly with his sandwich.

"Hoot died?" Will asked.

"He lost a leg and bled out at a gas station. That's quite a shotgun you've got, Dolly," Xavier commented.

Shep coughed, choking on a Dorito. Dolly pounded him on the back.

Xavier's eyes narrowed. "Milton, did you kill that man?"

"Yes, Dad," Shep replied once his throat was clear. "I was just going to kneecap him, but I was using his gun, and he must have had hollow-points or something in it because it blew his leg off at the knee instead."

"Great. Just great." Xavier pinched the bridge of his nose. "Okay. That I can deal with. This price on your heads is going to be a hell of a problem."

"Were those good cops that Hoot killed? It sounded like they were after the ransom, too," Will said.

"I wouldn't be surprised. Most of them didn't exactly have clean jackets," Xavier sighed. "Let's not worry about that now. I need to figure out where I'm going to keep you two until I can get you to a proper hearing."

"That proved quite an undertaking for those who were in charge of Caleb and Jacey Killeen," Will reminded us all.

"My parents," I added.

"I know." Xavier rubbed the bridge of his nose again. "I know. On the one hand, you two falling into my lap is like mana from the sky. On the other, we could all get killed for helping you."

I looked at Dolly and Shep. "You should go now. Thank you for your help, but I don't want you two to die."

Dolly drew herself up, and I could tell she was gearing up to give me what for, but Shep put a hand on her shoulder.

"That was always the plan, Mama. Get them here and get out of it," he said.

"I'd prefer it that way as well," Xavier added. "I love you, Milton. And I love you, Dolly, despite circumstances keeping us apart. I don't want anything to happen to you. And this situation is too hot for any of us to handle. I still don't know how *I'm* going to handle it. But, as a law-abiding judge…."

"Who wants a place on the Supreme Court," Dolly inserted.

Xavier frowned. "*As* a law-abiding judge, I have to do something about this. It's my duty."

Dolly grunted but finally gave in with a sigh. "Fine. We'll go. But if Felicity does anything to fuck this up, Xavier, so help me God…."

"Yes, I know. You're going to twist my balls off. I believe you," Xavier said.

Shep helped his mother out of her chair. "Good seeing you again, Dad."

"Still wish you would do something more meaningful with your life than being a trucker, Milton. You did so well on the LSAT…" Xavier lamented.

Shep just laughed good-naturedly, stroking his bushy beard. "Trust me, trucking's a lot better than what you've got going on here. Good luck to you."

"I'm going to need it," Xavier muttered.

"You remember the name Milton Pope if you ever get into trouble," Shep murmured to us. "Ask any trucker on the road, and they'll find me." Then he put a hand at Dolly's back and ushered her out of the office.

Xavier visibly relaxed. "All right, you two. I've assembled a team in the conference room. I didn't want to tell Dolly and Milton because I didn't want them to be targeted. The fewer people who know about this, the better. Let's go."

We rose and followed him.

Xavier pushed open the conference room doors, but instead of a team of people, there was only one. A dark-haired, swarthy man in a suit.

"Well," the man said. "Aren't you two cuter than a puddle of puppies."

"Ibrahim." Will swore.

26
BONUS CHAPTER: TROUBLE

Caleb

I sat on the deck of the cabin we'd bought secretly years ago under our false identities. We'd hoped never to have to use it, but the caretaker we'd hired to look after it left it in perfect condition.

My laptop balanced on my knees—yet another item purchased under another man's name. Chris Palmer. *I am now Chris Palmer.*

Jacey—or, rather, Janice—almost scared me right out of my Adirondack chair when she appeared next to me with two cups of coffee. But then, I'd already been scared by what I was reading online.

"What?" she asked, sitting down next to me in the other chair and setting the coffees on the small wooden table between us. "What's wrong?"

"McKenzie's not at school," I began, trying to formulate how to say this to my wife. Jacey had a good head on her shoulders, but she was also a mother, just like I was a father. And I was already panicking.

She froze. "She what now?"

I guessed there was nothing for it. I turned the laptop in my lap so Jacey could see. "McKenzie's wanted for murder."

"*What?!!!*" She snatched the laptop out of my hands and skimmed the article that had our smiling daughter's face at the top next to the thirty-year-old man who'd come to our home and sent us running.

The thirty-year-old Will Masterson the Third.

I should have recognized him the moment I saw him. He looked so much like his father, God rest his soul.

"Cops?! Our daughter murdered *cops*?!" Jacey cried incredulously.

"Keep reading," I murmured. I didn't think I'd be able to tell her the rest past the unexpected lump in my throat.

My wife kept reading. I knew the moment she saw it when she turned absolutely white. "S-Sam?"

"It looks like Hank, Mom, and Sam are dead, sweetheart," I croaked. I tried to clear my throat, but it didn't work.

"Oh God." The laptop slid from her fingers, and I just barely managed to catch it before it hit the decking. "What does that make now?"

"Well, with what happened at the farm, and Jake, the cops, our f-family, and then there's a mention in there about a wanted assassin they were traveling with named Hoot. The body count is rising," I said softly.

Jacey squared her shoulders. "It's our body count. Not hers. Damn Masterson anyway!"

"Love, it's *his* body count, not anyone else's. Masterson did this, I'm sure of it. I'll bet Will came to us for help, and we took off on him. I suppose it was only natural he'd latch onto McKenzie," I thought things through aloud.

"Well, pardon me for saying so, but I sort of wish this Will was a little more helpless and had left McKenzie out of it," my wife sighed.

I raised an eyebrow at her. "You'd rather he'd killed himself instead?"

Her shoulders drooped. "No. No, of course not. I... I really just wish we'd gotten custody of him."

"Me, too. But I don't think we could have disappeared well enough to evade Masterson all these years if we had," I pointed out.

Jacey raised her tearful gaze to mine. "Caleb, do you really think we managed to evade Masterson all these years if Will was able to just walk right up to our door? If he was able to find our parents and S-Sam?"

In my mind, it all clicked into place, and I groaned loudly. "He knew. He always knew."

She nodded. Then she covered her face with her hands and sobbed. "S-Sorry, I didn't think it would affect me this way if they died...."

"They're still our family," I said glumly. I reached around the steaming coffee and took her hand. "They're still our family, love. Of course we're going to be sad about it."

Jacey hiccuped then got out of her chair.

I put the laptop gently down beside me so she could scramble into my lap. I wrapped my arms around her and cuddled her close. "It's okay to not be okay," I assured her, a tear rolling down my cheek.

"I never thought we'd reconcile with them, or even see them again, but part of me hoped, I think," she choked, her tears wet against my shoulder. "And now we don't even know where McKenzie is, and she's in trouble, and there's nothing we can do!"

"What we know is that they haven't found her, and that's something," I said. I kissed her hair and rocked her a little. It was soothing to me, too.

She nodded again. "That's something," she echoed.

We stayed that way for a long time, the cool morning air swirling around us and rustling through the trees. It made our tears cold, but we cried anyway.

The coffee was long cold before she started wriggling out of my lap. "We need to figure out what to do," she said.

"Do?" I frowned slightly. "What do you mean 'do'?"

"We can't just sit here in this cabin while our daughter is on the run," she decided. "We need to find her and get her to safety. Will, too."

I could think of a million problems with that line of thinking. She picked up the coffees and headed purposefully inside. I scooped up the laptop and closed the sliding door behind us. "Jacey," I started patiently.

"Don't try to tell me why we can't do anything. This is our daughter we're talking about, and clearly she is in a lot of danger," she grunted, dumping the cold coffee into the sink.

"Jacey, baby, we don't know where she is. And Masterson has killed every resource we had," I said slowly, trying to make her see sense. "If we come out of hiding, we're going to be used against her. It's not safe for us. It's not safe for her. It's not safe for Will."

She slapped her hands down on the edge of the sink. "Caleb, we can't just stay here and do nothing!"

"Right now, that's all we can do, love," I replied. "I'm not happy about it, but we don't have a choice."

"So, according to you, we're just going to sit here," she snapped at me.

I folded my arms over my chest. "No. According to me, we're going to keep watching and waiting and looking for our opportunity to act."

Jacey began scrubbing the cups angrily. She didn't want to hear reason, but she wasn't immune to it, either. "She's just nineteen years old."

"And he's thirty, clearly with a better head on his shoulders than his father, God rest him, and a bigger heart than his grandfather. Will has money. I'm sure he'll figure something out," I responded, and hoped I wasn't lying. In truth, I wanted to leave the cabin and start searching for my daughter, but there were a couple of problems with that, the first and most important being we didn't know where to begin looking. The second, well, we'd be putting her in more danger and not less just by being with her.

She eyed me askance. "You really think Will, after his fancy upbringing, is going to know anything about being on the run?"

"Well... no..." I blew out a long breath. "But that still leaves the money part. He has money. We didn't."

Jacey laughed bitterly. "You think there are any funds he might have that aren't controlled somehow by Masterson?"

I tried not to let that break my spirit, but she had a point. "A man smart enough to come looking for us is probably smart enough to keep some of his own accounts."

"So he thinks. I'll bet Masterson has them all tagged by now, just waiting for him to pull out funds." She shook her head. "Face it, Caleb. They're not any better off than we were."

I opened my mouth to try to poke holes in her fears when there was a knock at our door. We both stiffened reflexively, but then I saw it was just the caretaker holding our groceries.

"Quincy," I said, pulling open the door with a wide, fake smile on my face. "Thanks for bringing groceries today."

"That's my job," Quincy grinned, carrying the bags to the kitchen.

Instead of staying in the kitchen to put things away, however, Jacey all but sprinted over to me.

"What?" I asked quietly when she gripped my arm.

"I didn't ask Quincy to bring groceries, Caleb," she whispered to me.

My head snapped up to look at Quincy just as he drew a gun out of one of the bags and pointed it at us. "Sorry, folks," he said as I pushed Jacey behind me. "But I've got five hundred million reasons to keep you here until your ride arrives."

"Our ride?" I squeezed her wrist, encouraging her to run.

He fired at the floor next to us, and she squeaked. "Don't think I didn't see that. I'm getting all five hundred million. Every last cent."

"How did you find out about us?" I asked.

"I've got a friend who's a cop. He's coming to get you." He grinned at us and let out a low whistle. "Five hundred million bucks. We're gonna be rich."

"You mean I'm gonna be rich," a deep voice said from the doorway.

We turned just in time to see a strange man in a police uniform raise his gun and shoot Quincy in the head.

"Jesus Christ!" I yelled, grabbing Jacey against me and holding her in my arms.

"You can just call me Booth. Now, let's go get in the squad," he said, gesturing with his gun.

I kept an arm around Jacey as we walked out of the cabin. I gave thought to tackling the policeman so she could run, but then I noted a second squad outside the cabin.

Actually, there were no less than four squad cars lined up in my driveway.

"What the...?" Booth muttered when he walked out behind us.

"Booth, next time you tie your partner up and throw her in your trunk, your idiot brain might tell you to take her cell phone," a portly officer said, leaning against one of the squad cars with a frazzled woman with a blanket around her standing next to him.

"Fuck." Booth grabbed Jacey and ripped her away from me. "I'm leaving with this one." He put a gun to her head.

I saw red, equal parts terrified and enraged. "Let her go."

"Piss off, Killeen." Booth started backing up along the wraparound deck.

The portly officer sighed and spoke into his walkie-talkie. "Nick," was the only thing he said.

Booth's eyes widened just in time for him to suddenly lose his hand. It, and the gun in it, went flying away.

Jacey got splattered with Booth's blood and screamed, running back to me while Booth held the stump of his wrist, howling.

I locked my arms around Jacey and buried her face in my shoulder, not wanting her to see the grisly scene. "What the hell?!" I shouted.

"Booth," the portly officer said, ignoring me. "Unless you want to lose more than your hand, you're going to surrender right now."

With a growl of frustration, Booth whirled on the other officers. Eight guns, plus Nick's, wherever he was, pointed right at him. "Fuck, Val. It's five hundred million dollars!"

"And you took an oath. Seems you forgot it. Again." The portly officer inclined his head. "You coming quietly? I might not throw you in the trunk of my squad."

Booth's shoulders sagged, and he plodded down the front steps of our cabin, letting someone treat his wrist while another officer patted him down.

"You two can come here, too. Obviously, this place isn't safe for you anymore," Val said.

I scooped Jacey up in my arms and walked down the steps, eyeing every one of the officers. Who would be tempted? Would they all start shooting each other, trying to get the ransom for themselves?

Val opened the back of his squad car, and my stomach dropped when I saw the standard bars between us and the driver and passenger. There would be no getting out of there once we got in. "We need to take you in to clear up a few things. Then the Attorney General is asking about you."

"It's not still her, is it?" I groaned, hoping a good twenty plus years had made a difference.

"Not the same lady as when you testified before, no. But still just as keen, I guess," Val said. "Seems you were supposed to go with Interpol after that Masterson trial. Pretty sure she's sending you overseas to complete that deal, but that's way above my pay grade."

My throat went dry. "Look, our daughter's in trouble...."

"Oh, you bet your sweet ass she is. That's why you're coming to the station. We need to know where she is," Val replied.

"We'd like to know that, too," Jacey said softly, her voice muffled by my shoulder.

ALSO BY M. FRANCIS HASTINGS

Once Bitten

Submitting to My Stepbrother series

Stranded With My Stepbrother

Snatched With My Stepbrother

Sequestered With My Stepbrother

Subpoenaed With My Stepbrother

Flirting With the Forbidden

The Beguiling Baronets series

Deceiving the Duke

Dream Mates

Dream Weaver

Dream Reader

Sign up for my newsletter here: https://subscribepage.io/TfsA3A

www.ingramcontent.com/pod-product-compliance
Lightning Source LLC
Chambersburg PA
CBHW052030121224
18825CB00051B/54